Eric Flint's 1632 & Beyond
Issue #9

1632 and Beyond, George Grant, Terry Howard, Marc Tyrell, Garrett W. Vance, Tim Sayeau, Iver P. Cooper

Flint's Shards, Inc.

ERIC FLINT'S 1632 & BEYOND ISSUE #9

Editor-in-Chief Bjorn Hasseler
Production and Design Bethanne Kim
Editor Chuck Thompson
Cover Artwork from Gerard ter Borch (Gerard Terburg), Dutch, 1617-1681.
Interior Art Garrett W. Vance

1. Science Fiction-Alternate History
2. Science Fiction-Time Travel

eBook ISBN: 978-1-962398-21-3
Paperback ISBN: 978-1-962398-22-0

Distributed by Flint's Shards Inc.
339 Heyward Street, #200
Columbia, SC 29201

Contents

Eric Flint's 1632 & Beyond Issue #9

The Magdeburg Messenger
(1632 Fiction)

This issue's cover is for "Unintended Consequences." It's barely longer than flash fiction, and George Grant has written a profound in-universe look at what the Ring of Fire means. It's also first because "Unintended Consequences" is a fair description of all the stories in this issue.

"Bremen Or Bust" was first printed in Terry Howard's *The Legend Of Jimmy Dick*. We are republishing it because it's a good story in its own right, and it sets up an upcoming storyline.

Marc Tyrrell's "Family Matters" shows that although the Ring of Fire didn't magically make family issues go away, it did provide new—or old—ways of dealing with them.

Sometimes what seems like a quiet shift of guard duty changes lives. Find out how in Garrett W. Vance's "The Rice Farmer's Daughter And The Samurai."

"Rose-Hip And Red Velvet" by Tim Sayeau is the sequel to "A Guest At The New Year" in Issue 6. Sir William and Dame Dorothy reply to Adina's letter.

State Library Papers
(Non-Fiction)

One piece of up-time technology has appeared here and there in stories. In "X-Rays," Iver P. Cooper explains how they work and what might be available in the new timeline.

Editors' Notes

Eric Flint's 1632 & Beyond is making some changes.

As most of our readers know, *Eric Flint's 1632 & Beyond* is a successor to the *Grantville Gazette*, a short-story venue created by Eric Flint. The *Gazette* was forced to close after Eric died, but one year later, Issue 1 of the new magazine was published. The primary change was removing the "Annex" with science fiction stories unrelated to anything Eric Flint wrote and a resulting shorter word count.

The new venture came with a new team, but it was built on the old team. The Managing Editor of the Gazette, Bjorn Hasseler, stepped up to be the Editor-in-Chief. Two writers, Bethanne Kim and Chuck Thompson, stepped up to take care of a variety of other tasks, including the website, accounting, contracts, etc. When their skill sets were combined, it left one very large, very glaring hole: artwork. So, they made a call to the man who had been Art Director since Volume 16 of the Gazette, Garrett W. Vance. Garrett had a new day job that consumed most of his time, but his response was, "We're getting the band back together?!?" And like that, he was back, creating a new logo, covers, story banners, and whatever else was needed.

But he still had that pesky day job. Continuing to do the job of Art Director left him with no time to write new stories for either *1632* or *Time Spike*. A year after he signed on, everyone sat down and had a conversation, the end result of which was that Garrett stopped making the time-consuming cover art and stepped down as Art Director. He is now focused on writing his stories and creating all the story banners.

Garrett, thank you for all the many wonderful covers and bits of artwork you have created. We look forward to more artwork and stories from you.

For the rest of us, this means that the covers will look different going forward, with stronger historical elements. The story banners won't change. And Grantville will finally have soy sauce once Garrett's characters arrive from Asia.

Helen Monath joins the staff as assistant editor. She has been one of the proofreaders for *1632 & Beyond*. Helen took the lead on one story last issue and two stories this issue.

As we attend conventions and interact with other writers and publishers online, we hear good ideas. A tip of the hat to Raconteur Press: They've announced "25 in '25." For each of their anthologies, they've posted the theme, the opening and closing dates for submissions, the date contracts are sent, and the publication date.

1632 & Beyond publishes on the first day of odd-numbered months: January 1, March 1, May 1, July 1, September 1, and November 1. In 2025, some of our issues will have a theme:

Issue 10 (March 1): Spies – 2025's 1632 Con will be at Fencon in Dallas on February 14-16. The convention has a theme of Spy vs. Spy, and this issue publishes just a couple of weeks later. Please see fencon.org and join us if you can

Issue 12 (July 1): Redbird Institute – This is the new timeline's version of the Chautauqua Movement: camp, STEM, the arts, itinerant lecturers.

We anticipate these stories will share the camp location and some characters. It's a higher degree of coordination between writers than usual.

Issue 15 (January 1, 2026): Romance – Yes, this is a full year away, but it's January 1, so writers need some lead time.

The others (11, 13, and 14) will be regular issues. We want to make sure writers have plenty of chances to tell the stories they want to tell.

In Memoriam

Flint's Shards, Inc.

Joseph (Jody) Dorsett

Jody Dorsett passed away in July. He was known as Quilly Mammoth on Baen's Bar. He was a Lutheran pastor. When large numbers of Pokémon players came to the church property, Jody's solution was to put out bottles of water and church flyers for them.

He wrote "The Three R's" in the first Ring of Fire anthology. That one story introduced the Hussites/Unitas Fratrum/Bohemian Brethren and Jan Comenius. This helped set up Eric Flint's short novel "The Wallenstein Gambit." It's had far-reaching consequences since then, ranging from Comenius' attendance at the Besançon Colloquy to the Bohemian Brethren's presence in *1637: The Transylvanian Decision*.

I met Jody in person once, outside the overflow hotel for Libertycon in 2015. He'd just parked his motorcycle. Jody wanted to send one of the Bohemian Brethren to North America and said he knew just the rest area welcome center for a Grantviller to have picked up a pamphlet with a Cherokee syllabary.

Jody is survived by his son, Tripp.

Magdeburg Messenger
1632 Fiction

Flint's Shards, Inc.

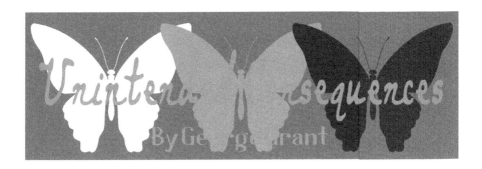

Unintended Consequences
George Grant

Boston
May 1635

Mr. Roger Ludlow looked around his new office with satisfaction. While cruder than anything he would have inhabited in England, as far as he was concerned it was the best there was in the New World. He had achieved his highest ambition. Last year he had been elected Deputy Governor of the Colony of Massachusetts Bay; just a few days ago he had defeated John Haynes in a close election to become its Governor. Now he was in the office he had long coveted.

Someone knocked on the door. Mr. Ludlow called out, "Enter," and the door opened to reveal Henry Vane carrying a packet.

Vane approached Ludlow, holding out the packet as he came. "A ship arrived from Europe this morning, carrying this. It is addressed to you."

Ludlow took it. "Thank you." As Vane left, he looked at the fat brown envelope. It had an unusually smooth quality, and the writing on it had been made using no pen he was familiar with. He turned it over and discovered a small bit of shiny metal attached to the flap at one end. Picking up a knife, he slit that end of the envelope and removed its contents. There was a cover letter on top of a booklet.

The letter read:

Dear Mr. Ludlow,

I am a scholar in Grantville, the town from the future that I'm sure you have heard about. There are a lot of events in the near future we know about because they happened in our past—but because we are here, things won't happen the same way as they did the first time. We would like to prevent some events, but others are important and we would like to ensure they happen the same way or better.

You were a critical contributor to one of those things. After you lost the 1635 gubernatorial election to John Haynes—which you may well have by the time this reaches you—you reversed your position on the matter of emigration to Connecticut and, shortly thereafter, went yourself. Several years later, in 1638 and 1639, you wrote the Fundamental Orders of Connecticut establishing a new government for Connecticut Colony. It was the first written constitution in the world and established the pattern for the constitutions of several other states and nations. It was instrumental in the move toward constitutional democracy worldwide.

I am concerned that, with all the changes the people of

Grantville have caused, the Fundamental Orders might not get written, or written as well. Besides your own contributions, much of it was based on a sermon by Reverend Thomas Hooker establishing the theological basis for democracy. He didn't give that sermon until 1638, so it might not happen now. Given all that, I have enclosed a copy of the Fundamental Orders for you in case you need it when the time comes

Also, during your tenure as Head Magistrate of the Commission for Connecticut in 1636, you established the principle of allowing those not of the local religion to join the community anyway, another important development in the governance of the future. Please be sure to do these things again!

Sincerely,

Robert Davidson

Ludlow set the letter down on his desk and leaned back in his chair to think without even glancing at the rest of what this "scholar" had sent him.

So, he had lost the recent election for governor in their world, had he? Had immediately turned to face the other way regarding emigration, and gone to Connecticut himself? And then joined a rebellion against the godly government of Massachusetts Bay just a few years later? For that was the only thing this scholar could have meant by his assertion that Ludlow had established a new government for Connecticut Colony.

One of the most vexing questions facing Massachusetts right now was whether to allow emigration. He had been opposed to it right along, but recognized the difficulty of keeping everybody from leaving. He had been willing to seek an accommodation as long as those who went continued to submit themselves to the authority of God's rule in Boston. But here was evidence that in merely three years emigrants to the Connecticut River Valley would start a successful rebellion against Massachusetts Bay. That would not do.

Even before then, he would evidently have been convinced—undoubtedly by those same rebels—to allow the pollution of God's people by permitting those with erroneous religious views to live side by side with God's own children. He had been accused in the past of having too liberal church views. He was sure his adoption of stricter views was part of what had won him the recent election, so he wasn't about to let himself be seen as liberal ever again. No, he must maintain strict church doctrine. And emigration must not be allowed, but be prevented at all cost. Reverend Hooker, now, that matter would take some thought. But there was time for that.

Governor Ludlow walked over to the fireplace with the envelope and its contents, dropped the booklet in the fire, and watched sparks fly up as flames began to curl around its edges. Nobody could ever be allowed to see such a dangerous document.

THE END

Grantville
Fall 1634

Sarah Beth Cochran was sitting behind her scarred wooden desk in her Social Studies classroom at the high school. She set Robert Davidson's story down on her desk and, like the Ludlow character in the story, leaned back in her chair. She had assigned the exercise titled "Write a story illustrating the Butterfly Effect" expecting the usual student twaddle. But this one—out of all of them, only this one—really drove the point home more than anything she had ever read or heard. It really showed how severely the Ring of Fire could—would—impact history and how up-timers needed to think about their effects on the world. Those effects even included possible negative consequences of actions that were intended to have a positive impact.

And Rob's story had not merely taken out the Connecticut Colony and the Fundamental Orders with it. It had irretrievably altered that other—and, truth to tell, more famous—wellspring of the American Experiment, Boston. Given the timing, Rhode Island was also at risk in the story.

Ms. Cochran was not the sort to give her students high praise. But now she sat up straight and tried to think of an adequate comment to go with the A+ grade the story was getting.

Bremen Or Bust

Terry Howard

Grantville
Friday evening, December 23, 1634

On Christmas Eve, white-haired, skinny as a rail Asa, and gray-haired, frail, and nearly emaciated Dory, dressed in their pajamas, were ready for bed. Wrapped in bathrobes, they sat on the French Provincial couch in front of the fireplace with its glazed Italian tiles and roaring fire. The imported tiles of the small, eighteen-nineties vintage, one bedroom house complemented the ornate oak woodwork. The two of them sipped a fine old Amontillado out of her grandmother's crystal stemware, as they had almost every Christmas Eve for nearly fifty years. They had just exchanged gifts. They slept in on Christmas day. He had given her a new set of boots and several pairs of warm socks. Her feet were getting wet walking to the tram to and from school now that she had temporarily come out of retirement. She gave him a fired clay building.

She thought she had the perfect Christmas present. A perfect present needed to be three things. First, it must be something the person wants. They may not have known it exists, but when they find out it does, they want it. Second, it should be something they would not buy for themselves. Third, it must be a surprise. Years ago, he had started collecting a Christmas village, and they had added to it year by year. Now, of course, there was no catalog to supply them. She showed a potter a picture of what she wanted and one of the buildings they already had, then rejected several firings until he made something close to what she wanted. Unfortunately, the fat-fingered Hungarian put the rejects on display. Asa saw them in the shop's window.

"I'm sorry, Asa. I really thought I had you surprised this year."

"It was sweet of you, dear. It really does look like it is part of the set. I'm sorry I got you something practical. But it was all I could think of." He had taken an old pair of shoes down to the shoemaker. The cobbler made the lasts to fit the shoes, then he made the boots to fit the lasts. They were the best fitting, and perhaps the best made, shoes she had ever had. Still, it was not a particularly romantic present.

"Asa, there is only one thing in the whole wide world you could give me which I actually want."

They had three girls who didn't live in Grantville and missed them dearly. But presumably they were safe back up-time. Dory and Asa had thought about adopting more children when they were younger but really didn't think they could afford it. They thought about it again when the Ring of Fire moved them to Germany but decided it would not be fair to take on children they would not live to see grown. It was a loss they had buried so deeply they didn't even think about it. He knew exactly what she was talking about. They had traveled some when he was in Germany in the army. One of the places they went was Bremen. The story of the musicians of Bremen was a favorite of Dory's. The statue in the town of the animals standing on each other's backs caught her imagination at the time. It had been a life-long dream to go back.

They had planned to go several times but, each time, something came up. In 1970, they hadn't saved up the money. In 1980, the roof blew off the house, and the furnace went out. When that happened, Dory sighed and said, "It looks like our trip to Europe is gone with the wind." A decade later, Asa was in the hospital.

"We had the reservations made, Dory. The money is still in the bank. We would have gone. I know how much it meant to you."

"We could still go."

"Dory! Remember?" Asa sighed. He hated starting any conversation with the word "remember," but it was happening more and more often. "It's 1634. In a few days, it will be 1635. There's no airlines to take us there."

"Asa, we're already in Germany. We don't need an airline."

"Dory." Asa sighed again. "I'll be seventy-five next month. You just turned seventy-two. Neither one of us is in what you would call good health. There is no way we can go traipsing off halfway around the world at our age."

"It's not halfway around the world." Dory put her glass down and folded her knurled, arthritic hands in her lap. When she did, Asa knew he was in for an argument. "It's less than a hundred and fifty miles as the crow flies. I've checked. We walked farther than that when we hiked the Appalachian Trail."

"We weren't seventy-two and seventy-five at the time, and it was in America where it was safe."

"It was safe?" Dory's hands did not move from her lap. But she raised a single eyebrow in a studied gesture. "Is that why you insisted on carrying a pistol?"

"Dory, it's out of the question. There's a war on. And even if there weren't you have to think about the bandits. On top of everything else, it's not like we can hop in the car and be there in two or three hours, no matter how fast I drive. A trip like that could kill us."

"Asa, you know I'm losing my mind."

"You're getting Alzheimer's; it's not the same thing as losing your mind."

"You can call it whatever you want. My memory is slipping. In another year or two, I may not know what day it is. I might not even know who you are. Just like my mother and my grandmother at the end. If the trip kills me, what will I lose? A handful of years of being tied to a bed down at the nursing home so I don't wander out into the snow and forget how to get back in. Back in 1970, Asa McDonald, you promised you would take me. I don't care that there isn't a highway. I want to see Bremen again before I die. It is less than two hundred miles away by road. Are you going to take me or am I going by myself?"

"You can't do that!" Asa raised his voice sharply.

"You just watch me."

"You'll get yourself killed."

"Then I'll die trying!"

"For crying out loud, woman, be reasonable!"

"Mr. McDonald. I have been reasonable my whole life. What has it gotten me? In another year or two, I won't be able to remember. It's all falling in on itself even as we speak. Husband, give me something to remember. My mother and her mother both ended up talking about the same thing over and over again each and every day. Give me something interesting to talk about. Take me to Bremen. You promised!"

When she picked up her glass, Asa knew the argument was over.

Noon, Monday, January 3, 1635

"Herr McDonald!" Anna, the young blonde secretary/receptionist, sat behind the old, gray steel desk in the front office of the machine shop. David Marcantonio paid ten dollars for the desk in a Salvation Army thrift store years ago when he started the business. A customer offered him a small fortune for it early in 1632. He decided to sell it when he found out he could buy a newly made hardwood desk of the same size or larger and still have money left over. When he mentioned this, the furniture maker offered a swap of two for one. Well, if they could give him two desks and still make money on it, that put a stop to the first deal. Every year since, he'd had two or three offers for the up-time desk, and the price kept going up. So, a beautiful young blonde sat behind the ugly piece of junk that continued in use. David didn't need the money. The shop was more than busy.

Anna was dressed in a thick sweater to ward off the chill, which radiated through the single-pane glass of the office's picture window. "It is freezing out there." She scolded the white-haired man with a cane as he limped from the shop door towards the front door and the street. "You must not go out without your coat and hat. You will catch pneumonia and die. If you are not here, what will Herr Marcantonio do the next time he cannot figure out how to do something and needs to know how the old-timers used to do it?"

Her last phrase was what Asa McDonald was noted for, remembering obsolete processes from the old days.

"Dave will figure it out without me if he has to. I'm just running across the street, Anna. I don't need my coat."

"And you are not wearing your boots! There is ice on the road. What will happen if you fall and break your hip? Who will look after your wife?

She is getting forgetful and needs you even more than Herr Marcantonio does."

"That's rather personal. Just who have you been talking to, girl?" The smile in his voice softened the harsh words.

Anna ignored the question. The lives of the up-timers were grist for the rumor mill in Grantville. Dory McDonald's pending Alzheimer's and the school's decision not to renew her contract for next year were common knowledge. "You wait there, and I will fetch your hat and coat from the time clock."

"That's okay. I'm just running across the street." And with those words, he left through the steel front door, which also had a standing offer if David ever wanted to sell it.

The wind-chill made its effect known, and Asa's shoes slipped on the ice, as he trod the asphalt between the two standard, cinder block industrial buildings. "You old fool. You should have let her go get your coat. She's right. Dory needs you."

* * *

"Wesley, how's business?" Asa asked as he approached the counter. The sign on the picture window at his back read "Pomal Conversions" in a recently touched-up crisp Gothic script in royal blue with gold highlights. The walls inside and out had been painted late in the summer and were still neat and pristine. Across the street the sign painted on the window in the dirty whitewashed cinderblock building announced that it was Marcantonio's machine shop. The script was plain, and the paint was faded. But, with more work than he could handle, Dave Marcantonio wasn't overly worried about making a good first impression.

"Staying busy." The much younger but balding, dark-haired Wesley Pomeroy replied proudly. More than once since the Ring of Fire he had feared that he would not be able to keep the door of his shop open, van conversion being, at least at first glance, a distinctly up-time business.

He did not have to look up more than an inch to make eye contact with the six-foot-two still-shivering machinist. "What can I do for you, Mr. McDonald?"

Asa opened a manila folder and put a pile of drawings as thick as a nickel on the counter, leaving slightly oily fingerprints on the top and bottom sheets. "It's pretty straightforward."

Wesley thumbed through them. His hands left no visible smudge even though there was a black line ingrained around his fingernails and in the creases of his knuckles from working on dirty engines.

"Asa, if this is straightforward, I would hate to see what you call complicated. But then if you admit that it's complicated, you can't argue it should be done cheaply." The top one showed a VW minibus exterior, converted to a coach and six. It was a different sort of van conversion than Wesley did up-time, but it was still a conversion. Wesley nodded. It was what he was doing for a living these days, converting up-time automobiles to horse-drawn carriages, mostly for rich down-time nobles who wanted to show off just how much money they had to throw away. It was profitable work, and it kept him in business, since the conversion of cars and tractors from unleaded to natural gas, which kept him busy right after the flash of light, was pretty much over.

"You've got a driver's seat on the roof and a slot under the window for the reins."

"I like options." Asa pointed to the next picture, "I want the two front bucket seats on turntables so they can face forward to drive or backwards to ride and chat with other passengers."

Wesley nodded again.

"Now this's interesting," Wesley said, pointing to a drawing of a generator and a hydraulic pump being turned by the drive axle to feed a series of batteries and a power fluid system where the engine used to sit.

"Just because the engine went to the Air Force, I don't see why I should give up on the lights or the electric heater. I paid extra for the heater. I want to use it. I want the brakes working too, at least while the bus is moving. The handbrake can hold it when it's standing still. I'll supply the parts. All you have to do is install the system." He flipped to the next page. "You can see we will want a second set of brake controls for the seat up top."

"Have you thought of how much drag that is going to add?" Wesley asked.

"No."

"I think you will find it's not a good idea."

"Well, I want to try it, at least."

Wesley nodded. "You're paying for it. Now this here," Wesley said, pointing at the front axle. "Mostly we've been pulling the front suspension and putting in a hay trailer axle. You've got us tying into the existing system."

"It will work."

"Cost a lot to get it made, though."

"I'll make up the parts. All you have to do is install it when you pull the steering wheel. I've seen what you usually do. It works fine, but you have to cut the old wheel wells away for the thing to turn. This"—Wesley wrapped his knuckles on the next picture—"will look better, it keeps the springs intact, and I get to keep those fancy air-filled shock absorbers I had put on."

"Well, if we cut it away, we can move the lights up to the top to shine over the horses," Wesley said.

Asa rubbed his jaw. "I hadn't thought—no, leave them, I've got the front lights off of a 1932 Ford 'B' Model in the rafters over the garage. They were there when we bought the place, and I never bothered taking them down. Let's leave the lights where they are for aesthetics and mount those up top."

"Do they still work?" Wesley asked.

"If they don't, we can use the housings and have them rewired."

"I suppose you want this tomorrow." Wesley unconsciously rubbed his temple to massage a headache that was not there, as he started to marshal the reasons why it couldn't be done quickly.

"No." Asa forestalled Wesley's thoughts with a dismissive wave of his hand. "No hurry. Middle of next month will be fine."

"I see. You've got rigging for a six-horse team and a full luggage rack over the whole roof behind the driver's seat. You don't need six horses here in town. Are you going into passenger service or something?"

"We're going to be doing some traveling come late spring after the weather clears."

"Oh, where are you going?"

"My wife wants to go to Bremen."

"Bremen? I guess that makes sense the way she has always loved it. She told us all about it when I had her for a teacher. She told us the story of the Musicians of Bremen and showed us the picture of the statue. And then she told us all about how she went to Germany when you were in the army after your tour in Korea."

"Yeah," Asa said, "that was a long time ago. We got married just before I shipped out for Korea. To get me to sign up for a second tour, they offered me a tour in Germany. But I said I wanted to go home to my wife, so they said I could bring a dependent over to Germany. Dory agreed, so I signed on for a second tour. There was just something about that statue in Bremen that she fell in love with. All these years she's wanted to go back. And now that we're here she says she's going."

Wesley asked, "Doesn't she know there's a war on?"

Asa winced. "There's a war on?" Asa asked, inflecting his voice to make the statement a question while bumping his forehead with the heel of his hand in mock surprise. "Really?"

Then in a calm voice, he said, "Trust me, Wesley. I tried that argument."

Wesley started to say something.

"I tried that one, too," Asa said before he even heard what the man was going to say. "She's got her mind made up. I can take her or she's going without me."

"Well, Mr. McDonald, if you've got to go, you've got to go. I've got to admit if I were going, especially at your age, I'd want the best ride I could get, and it looks like we will be getting that for you," Wesley said, tapping the pile of drawings.

Lisa Alcom, Wesley's partner and co-owner in the conversion business, came into the office from her section of the shop. The short, blonde-haired woman was as plump as her partner. They looked like a married couple even though they weren't. She handled the upholstering end of the business and the bookkeeping. He did everything else. Lisa looked at the top picture on the pile while the men were talking.

"I remember when I had your wife as a teacher," Lisa said. "She took one whole afternoon and told us all about her trip and the history of Bremen and the statue of the musicians." She didn't mention the student's bright idea of distracting their teacher with a question about it whenever someone didn't have their homework done. If you could get her started, she could and sometimes would talk all afternoon on the subject. It was nearly thirty years ago, but Lisa still felt a little guilty about it.

"Yeah. I remember it too." Wesley added, "Shoot, it was nearly fifty years ago. I was in the first class she ever taught. I still remember how excited she was and how exciting she made it sound. Shoot, I've dreamed of going myself."

"You and everybody else who ever had her for a teacher," Lisa said.

That evening Lisa told a girlfriend about Old Lady McDonald's planned trip. It would be an exaggeration to say everybody in town knew all about it by the next morning, but not by much.

* * *

Wesley helped his wife Sheryl, still in her white cooking apron with its red-tipped ruffled edges, put the pot roast dinner on the table. Sheryl was a good match for her husband's personality, but she was not at all a match for Wesley's build, being as she was on the skinny side. Since the Ring of Fire, in the absence of home hair dyes, Sheryl's hair had grown out gray, and she had it cut short, so it was all gray just as soon as the gray was long enough to let her do so without looking butch. She had taken to keeping it covered when it started growing out, and she still kept it covered even after she had it cut short. As he set the table, he told her about Asa putting in the order.

"Asa sold the motor out of his old VW bus to Jesse to make an airplane. So now he wants it rigged to be pulled by horses." Over dinner, he told her about Mrs. McDonald reading her class the story of the Musicians of Bremen and showing her third-grade class a picture of the statue in Bremen with the rooster standing on the cat, standing on the dog, standing on the donkey. "Then she told us about her trip and seeing the statue in person."

When he ran down, his wife looked at him and said, "You want to go, don't you!"

"Don't be ridiculous."

Sheryl put her fork down and focused her cornflower blue eyes on her husband's chubby face. "I'm not being ridiculous. You would like to go."

"I'd like to go to China, too!" he said with a laugh.

"Yes. But you can't go to China. You could go to Bremen. You've been dreaming of it your whole life ever since you were in the third grade. Admit it."

Wesley looked down at his plate, so Sheryl saw his horseshoe haircut instead of his blushing cheeks. "Honey, I've had a lot of dreams. I even wanted to be an astronaut once."

"So, you can't go to the moon. You could go to Bremen." She picked her fork back up and took a bite of the apple pie she had made for dessert.

"It's too dangerous."

"Wesley Pomeroy," Sheryl said with a touch of impishness in her voice—Wesley fell in love with it all those years ago when they were dating—"are you going to sit there and tell me you are ready to stand by and watch as those two old people do something you want to do but don't have the balls to even try?"

Well, when a fellow's wife puts it to him that way, what can a man say? He looked up, placed both palms on the table, made hard eye contact, and in a firm and no-nonsense voice asked, "Do you want your own coach or are we going to share theirs?"

"What?" She snorted. "What makes you think I'm going?"

"Sheryl Pomeroy, are you going to admit he loves his wife enough to go with her on the trip of a lifetime but you don't love your husband enough to do the same? Or are you hoping I'll get myself killed so you can sell the business and run off to Miami?"

She broke out in laughter. Her husband smiled in return. Every time they ever got into a fight about anything it always ended with her threatening to run off to Florida, especially since the Ring of Fire.

The next day Wesley stopped into the machine shop across the street from his business and wandered out onto the shop floor. He found Asa sitting on a stool watching a turret lathe do what a turret lathe does. Asa's walking stick, which he had cut from a young oak on the hillside, leaned against the stool. "Asa, the wife and I were wondering if we can ride with you to Bremen. If not, then I need to get two of these things built in time for the trip."

"Wesley," Asa said, looking so solemn that he would have looked sour if he had been anyone else, but being sour just was not in him. "I should tell you: I'm building this mostly to keep Dory happy. When it comes right down to the wire, I plan to ask for official permission, and I expect to get turned down. But yes, if we go you are more than welcome to ride with us."

Grantville
January 5, 1635

Around lunchtime, Wesley came through the green front door of Club 250. The almost forgotten smell of tobacco smoke hit him like a brick wall. Ken was selling the tobacco to fill pipes, a dollar a fill. If you didn't bring your own pipe or paper to roll your own cigarette, you could borrow a long-stemmed clay pipe kept in a jar on the back-bar. Ken broke about an inch off of the stem after each use so you got a clean mouthpiece each time. It was something he'd seen done at a black-powder rendezvous once.

Tobacco had come close to disappearing after the Ring of Fire, and now it was shipped in at very high prices. It wasn't the mild tobacco of up-time cigarettes. There was a lot of research and development in the tobacco industry that got passed over when Grantville came back in time. But it was what there was. Wesley hadn't smoked before the Ring of Fire. He sang solos in the high school choir and now in the Methodist choir. Smoking cut into your wind, so he never took it up. He had never thought about how much he didn't miss it until Ken started selling it. Now his reaction was a wrinkled nose. "Why does anyone put up with it?"

He started to leave, but a voice called out, "Hey, Wes. Let me buy you a beer." The voice was James Richard Shaver's. Since Jimmy Dick owned the building Wesley ran his business out of, Wesley thought better of leaving.

Jimmy Dick looked odd to Wesley with a short haircut after decades of wearing it pulled back in a ponytail. The Vietnam Vet perched on a bar stool in jeans, a button-down white shirt, and an old, tan, Mr. Roger's-style cardigan sweater, with pockets, that the drunken reprobate wore from fall to spring. There was an empty stool on each side of the man while the rest were full. Jimmy Dick's notoriety for being a loud-mouthed, obnoxious, annoying drunk was hard-earned, well-deserved, and not soon forgotten.

Wesley found himself wondering just how it was that Jimmy Dick could spend all day, every day, drinking beer and still stay as skinny as he did. There didn't seem to be an ounce of fat on the man anywhere. Up-time, Wesley had to watch what he ate. It was a never-ending struggle to keep from bloating up like a blowfish. The first winter after the Ring of Fire there wasn't much extra, and he managed to lose weight. Now there was enough of a surplus to make plenty of beer, and Wesley had to watch it. Every time he had a beer it seemed to go right to his waist.

Wesley exposed his horseshoe haircut when he took off his stocking cap and stuffed it in his pocket. As he hung the coat he wore over his coveralls on a wall peg by the door he said, "Sure, Jimmy. A beer is what I came in for."

Ken set two newly made dark glass bottles on the counter. Beer bottles were amongst the first things the local glass industry turned out. As soon as someone imported cork, a tinker started making caps, and newly bottled beer was back with the return of the church key. Bottles from up-time were collectible and pretty much worth their weight in gold by this time.

Bottled beer was nearly synonymous with cold beer in Grantville; a glass or mug usually meant room temperature beer out of a keg. Drinking out of the bottle was practically a fashion statement or a declaration of culture. If you didn't want to drink out of the bottle, you had to ask for a glass in Club 250 these days. If you did, you ran the risk of being teased for being a sissy, or worse, a kraut lover.

"Burger, Wes?" Ken asked, as Wesley approached the bar.

Wes nodded.

"Fries?" Ken asked.

Wes shook his head no. Fries were expensive, and Ken's prices reflected that fact; they cost more than a hamburger did. On top of that, they were fried in lard and even worse for putting weight under his belt than beer.

When Wesley's bottom interfaced with the vinyl-covered foam-padded seat of the bar stool, Jimmy said, "I hear you're taking Old Lady McDonald to Bremen."

Jimmy turned the bottom of the bottle he was working on to the tin tray ceiling to get the last few drops. The genuine antique ceiling came from the same closed tavern as the dark wood bar, mirrored back-bar, and brass cash register. The building holding the hundred-year-old ceiling was less than fifty years old, and the bar had been in the building for the last twenty years.

"Well, I'm converting Asa's minibus to horse power for the trip, but I don't think they'll actually go," Wesley answered before he took a small sip. He limited himself to one or two beers a week in his battle of the bulge so when he drank beer, he drank them slowly to savor every drop.

"Ain't how I heard it!" Jimmy Dick snorted, reinforcing his words by plunking his empty bottle down hard on the bar and grabbing the new one, in a continuous motion which left his hand empty for only a fraction of a second. "What I heard was you were going with him."

Wesley's mind went back to the conversation with his wife. When it found its way back to where his bottom was squishing the foam of a vinyl covered bar stool, Wesley noticed Jimmy Dick staring at him.

"Earth to Wesley, over?" Jimmy Dick smirked.

"Well," Wesley told Jimmy Dick, "if Asa and Mrs. McDee do go, the wife an' I are going with them. But Asa said he doesn't think they will get to. He'll wait until the last minute and then ask for clearance. There's a war on you know. So it probably ain't safe."

"Shit, these days there's always a war on. If that were a consideration, nobody would ever go anywhere. So that's pure bullshit! I mean it, Wes. If Old Lady McDonald wants to go to Bremen, then damn it she should go! You tell Asa to forget about askin' for permission from the government. When she's ready to leave, there's enough of her students around willing to swat any bugs that get in the way to see to it the old lady gets there and back."

"You think there might be that kind of interest?"

"Shit yeah, of course, there is." Jimmy Dick continued, "I remember her telling us about it back in the third grade. She made it sound exciting. I've always thought I'd like to see it. If she wants to go, we'll get her there. You tell that to Mr. McDee. But Wesley, there's something I'm puzzled about." Jimmy took a swig of beer.

"Is the statue there yet? I mean, what's the point of going if it ain't?"

"I don't know," Wesley answered.

"Well," Jimmy Dick said when he set the beer down and wiped his mouth with the back of his sleeve, "it really doesn't matter. You tell Mr. McDee that if she wants to go to Bremen, we'll get her there."

Ken was back with the burger. It was lunchtime, and the patties were on the cast iron grill. It was winter, so there was no lettuce or tomato, but there were pickles and ketchup and mustard. Some people even made their own back before the Ring of Fire. Wes filled his mouth, taking note of the better-quality bun compared to what would have been commonly available before the flash of light. The wheat was a coarser grind than up-time, and it had more milk and eggs, so it was a heavier, darker bread. Light white bread was something else he didn't miss from up-time.

The door opened. Addison Miller came in. He was not a regular, but he had business with Jimmy Dick, and since Jimmy didn't keep a working phone and his mail was delivered to the office Addison worked in, catching Jimmy at the bar was just about the only sure way of getting a message to him. Jimmy called out, "Hey Ad, you had Mrs. McDonald for the third grade. We're putting together an escort to see her to Bremen in the spring. You in?"

"Don't know if the wife would let me do that."

"Wes here is taking his wife with him," Jimmy said.

"Jimmy," Wes said, "Don't you think we ought to ask Asa before you go making plans?"

"Shoot, Wes, what will it hurt to see who's interested?"

"I think you should wait and ask."

"Well, you check with Asa and get back to me."

Addison hopped up on the last empty barstool and Jimmy waved three fingers at the bartender.

"Jimmy, we've got a stack of papers for you to sign. And we got some mail you need to look at."

"I'll stop by when I get the time," Jimmy replied.

Wesley made an exception and had a second beer. When the burger was only a memory, he pushed the plate away and reached for his wallet.

"I've got it," Jimmy said. "You're a tenant. I can take it off my income taxes as a business lunch."

"Thanks, Jimmy. I'll check with Asa."

* * *

Of course, Jimmy Dick did not wait for a reply from Asa McDonald. By the time the bar closed for the night, anyone who came through who might be interested in helping "old lady McDee," and everybody who wasn't at all interested, for that matter, were all very aware that Jimmy Dick was organizing an armed escort for the McDonalds' spring trip to Bremen. The number of people who were, metaphorically, looking at their early summer schedules said a great deal for the quality of Mrs. McDonald as a person and as a teacher. The number of men who were reviewing their traveling gear and wardrobe said even more.

Grantville was never a very big place. The news that the McDonalds were going to Bremen had already penetrated to the saturation point before Wes and Jimmy had a beer over lunch. Jimmy's raising of an armed escort found its way to the last nook and cranny within forty-eight hours. By then, of course, the tale had only a passing acquaintance with facts. Up-time such would have been good for a chuckle and a comment on the credulity of gossips. But in the early winter of 1635, in Grantville, in the Germanies, gossip didn't stop at the back fence or the city limits.

* * *

"Hey?" Jimmy Dick asked Addison Miller, the office manager of Lamb Commercial Properties, as he walked into the office. "What ya' got for me?" They ran the business out of what had once been a first-class dwelling house on the edge of downtown when Victoria was Queen of England. Addison Miller now ran the business for Old Lady Lamb. He and Jimmy had been in Mrs. McDee's third-grade class, and they had graduated together. The draft sent Jimmy to Nam and tagged Addison as 4F. A relative of Jimmy Dick's started buying up downtown properties as business closed down. He left them all to Jimmy Dick while the boy was still in Vietnam, to the annoyance of the rest of the family. Owning the properties didn't mean squat before the Ring of Fire. After paying the taxes and upkeep and the fees to the management company, very little remained out of the rents. And nobody wanted to buy the buildings.

Everything changed with the Ring of Fire. Every roof had a family or three under it. One family to a bedroom with a shared bathroom and kitchen was a very common arrangement in Grantville now. Ground-floor business space was suddenly once again premium real estate. The rents were paying Jimmy's living, which was a good thing since his VA disability check stopped coming.

"Jimmy, we've got a stack of papers for you to sign. And we got some mail you need to look at."

"Shoot, Ad. If I owe it, pay it. If I don't owe it, tell them no."

"We told them no, but they keep saying they need to talk to you. There's three different private security groups who want to bid on providing security for your trip to Bremen."

"I bet that's the same people who keep sending notes to me at Club 250. Ad, tell them we ain't interested."

"One of them stopped in, and I told him. He just smiled and winked and said, of course, you need to hire a professional outfit. A ragtag group of amateurs isn't up to taking on a job of that size.

"Well, I told him it was just a tourist trip for a little old lady. He gave me a nod and left a business card. And he said, 'Tell Mister Shaver that we will be speaking to him.' Jimmy, are you sure you haven't gotten in over your head?"

"Yeah. Don't worry about it."

"Look, Jimmy, I know you haven't had a phone in years. But when we agreed to take care of your mail, we thought that might mean dealing with an occasional bill collector."

Addison held up a hand to forestall Jimmy's reply. "It hasn't ever happened. We pay your property taxes, and now we pay your gas bill when it comes in, and you don't hardly get any mail, so that's fine. After we pay the bills, we make a deposit at the bank, and everything is fine. But we never thought it would mean we'd have mercenaries showing up looking for you. We're not set up to handle that. The girls are all nervous and upset over it. I need you to take care of this, Jimmy."

"Okay, Ad. Send them a letter telling them to meet me at the Thuringian Gardens on the first of the month at noon. I'll get a private dining room and tell them to quit bothering you."

Family Matters

Marc Tyrrell

Chapman House, Grantville
Friday, June 4, 1632, 6:15 p.m.

"Do you know what that idiot brother of mine just did?!?" Gerald Chapman's voice was loud enough that everyone in the house, and probably most of the neighbors, could hear him. His wife, Leah, rolled her eyes as she stirred that night's dinner, simmering in the pot on the stove. "I can't believe that moron just mortgaged his house, rented it out, and is moving to Magdeburg to try and start a business."

Leah just shook her head. "If Ron wants to do that, it's his business. It's not like he has a wife and kids." She tasted the stew, grimaced, and added salt.

Gerry wasn't mollified. He paced back and forth in the kitchen, expounding on his brother's deficiencies. "Yeah, his choice, but who is going to have to pay when it all crashes, and he's penniless? Us! Why couldn't he have just gotten a job here! We both have jobs, and Ron, that slacker, thinks he can do better?" Gerry worked as a CNA at the Bowers Assisted Living Center, while his wife worked as a CNA at the Manning Assisted Living Center.

Gerry's rant continued, often devolving into scatological terms. Dave, his youngest son, could hear every word of it from two rooms away. Ah, crap! Dad's going to be on about this for months!

Chapman House
Monday, June 7, 1632, 2:35 p.m.

Dave closed the textbook he had been reading—well, trying to read—and gave out a sound halfway between a growl and a shriek. "I can't take this crap anymore." To Dave, summer school was just wrong, especially when he had to take German on top of a remedial science course.

His older brother, Tim, looked up from the textbook he was studying. "Dave, you really need to study up, otherwise there's no way you will get into medicine, even as a CNA."

Dave threw his hands up and rolled his eyes. "Does anyone in this house even listen to me? No! How often do I have to tell you, Tim, I don't want to go into medicine! Before the Ring of Fire, I wanted to be a mechanic. Now? Maybe something in steam engines or one of the machine shops. I just want to work with my hands. You know, make something."

Tim was nodding, with a wry smile on his face. "I know, little brother. But Dad wants you to follow in his footsteps and become a CNA." He shook his head. "I've had enough problems getting him to agree to let me train as an EMT after high school. He thinks I'm trying to 'get above myself.'"

Dave snorted "Yeah, well, at least you won't spend your life emptying bedpans, which is what he wants me to do." He leaned forward, "And let me tell you, I ain't doing that. No. Freakin'. Way!" He shoved the textbook away and glared at his brother, who just shrugged and went back to his own reading.

VoTech Center, Steam Workshop
Friday, June 11, 1632, 1:15 p.m.

Millard Barger was watching the kids in the class—at seventy-six years of age, anyone below sixty qualified as a "kid"—when he saw a youngster standing in the doorway, looking in longingly. He gave him a "come here" wave and, when he approached, asked, "What can I do for you, son?"

The youngster looked to be about eleven or twelve, with brown hair and standing about four foot six. "Uh, I'm Dave Chapman, sir."

Barger held out his hand. "Millard Barger. Don't think I know your family..." He frowned for a moment, then snapped his fingers. "Wait, are you one of Augie's grandkids?"

"Yes, sir."

Barger nodded. "How's he doing anyway? I haven't seen him for a couple of years, must be."

Dave's face grew long. "He, uh, didn't make it with us, sir."

Barger shook his head. "Drat. That's rough, son. My eldest boy, Quinn, got left up-time. I think the worst is just not knowing what's happened with them." He let out a sigh, then shook himself. "Well, no point in worrying about it, I guess. So, what can I do for you, Dave?"

Dave shifted nervously. "Well, sir, back up-time I wanted to be a mechanic or maybe a machinist. You know, working with my hands to make something." He shrugged. "Not much chance of that, for me at least, so I started reading up on steam, and it was really interesting. I had no idea that entire shops were run on steam, and it's something we can do now." Dave was starting to get enthused, then the enthusiasm drained away. "We won't even get to look at steam until high school, and my dad is pushing me to become a CNA, and not 'waste my time.'"

Barger was nodding. "Got your entire life planned out, does he?" At Dave's rather sullen nod, he continued, "How's your German? Mine's terrible; I never kept it up after I got home after the war."

Dave's eyes widened. "You were in World War II, sir?"

Barger shook his head. "Nah, just missed it. When I was drafted, I was in the Army of Occupation in '47 and '48. I picked up a bit but, as I said, I've lost most of it."

Dave nodded. "I'm learning it, but mostly what we are speaking at school is that weird English/German mixture."

Barger shrugged. "Better than me. Anyway, I'm in here every Friday afternoon, and I think I could use a volunteer translator. If you're interested." His eyes twinkled as Dave nodded his head rapidly.

VoTech Center, Steam Workshop
Friday, June 25, 1632, 2:45 p.m.

Millard Barger watched carefully as Dave adjusted the small steam engine he was helping to build. The kid's got the right attitude, he thought as he saw the way Dave was concentrating. A smile flitted over Millard's lips as he realized that Dave had only been showing up for two weeks, and he was already understanding how steam engines worked. Well, small ones at any rate. I wonder if I can get him out to the power plant to look at some of the big ones.

Dave backed away from the steam engine. "I think that's got it, Mr. Barger. What now?"

Millard smiled and said, "Now we figure out how we are going to hook it up and get some work out of it. So, if you were going to get it to power something, let's say a small hoist, how would you do it?"

Chapman House
Saturday, June 26, 1632, 2:25 p.m.

Gerald Chapman was in a foul mood as he walked through his front door. He had been on the early morning shift at Bowers, and it had been just one problem after another. The worst had been a down-timer with advanced Alzheimer's who was convinced that the staff were trying to kill him. He had become violent and had to be restrained after he attacked a nurse. Gerald had taken several punches during that encounter and was still hurting. Fucking Ring of Fire! Up-time, there would have been sedatives.

Glancing around, he saw his eldest boy, Tim, studying in the kitchen. "Where's Liz and Davey?"

Tim glanced up. "Liz is off with her friends. Dave is on a tour out at the power plant."

Gerald felt his frustration with Dave's lackadaisical attitude swirling like acid in his stomach. "What the hell is he doing out there? He should be studying and trying to get his marks up, not wasting his time sightseeing." Gerald glared at Tim. "And who the hell said he could go?"

Tim shifted to his calmest voice. "Mom signed the permission slip."

"Without talking to me?" Tim gave a small shrug. "Fine, I'll just have a talk with Davey when he gets back."

Two hours later...

Dave was feeling great as he walked through the front door, a feeling that drained out of him when he heard his father's voice coming from the living room. "Get your sorry ass in here, David." Oh, fuck! Dad's on another rampage!

Walking into the living room, he could see his father glaring at him from the couch. "Hi Dad. What's up?"

The glare deepened as he heard his father speak in a cold, angry voice. "Just what do you think you are doing wasting valuable study time? Your marks are shit, and I'm not going to let you slack off until you get them up." Gerald's voice increased in volume. "So here's the deal, David. You are grounded until your marks are higher. You only leave here to go to school, a family outing, or if you get a job, which I doubt you can, given what a slacker you are!"

By now, Dave was sure that the neighbors could hear every word. "But Dad, I..."

Gerald surged out of his chair and slapped Dave across the face, sending him reeling onto the floor. As he walked towards the prone Dave, he pulled off his belt. "I've told you before, no backtalk!"

11:25 p.m.

Dave's ass and face still hurt, and he was certain that he would have a black eye by morning. He quietly packed his knapsack in the room he shared with Tim, trying not to wake him, rolling up a blanket to take with him. He felt like crying but had no tears left. In reality, he felt nothing but despair, pain, and a desperate need to get away. Holding his shoes in one hand, he tiptoed out of the bedroom and down the stairs, leaving by the back door.

Chapman House
Sunday, June 27, 1632, 9:25 a.m.

Gerald looked up from his breakfast as Tim walked in. "Where's Davey?"

Tim shrugged. "Don't know. He wasn't in bed when I woke up. He's probably off somewhere."

Gerald frowned, and Leah started to look worried. "You were pretty hard on him yesterday, Gerry. He's probably off sulking."

Gerald glared at Leah. "Don't you start on me. I don't take backtalk from anyone."

Leah returned the glare, then smiled in a sickly sweet manner. "I'm so glad you remember '87. You do remember it, I assume?"

8:45 p.m.

Leah was pacing in the kitchen. She had spent the last hour calling the homes of Dave's friends, trying to find him without any luck. *I really don't want to call, but...I really need to find Dave.* She picked up the phone and dialed.

Briinnggg, bri... "Hello?"

"Summer? It's Leah Chapman calling."

The phone line was silent for a moment. "Hi, Leah. Uh, what's up?"

Leah snorted. "I'm sorry to bother you with this, but I know Bob and Gerry really don't talk." She shook her head. "Talk about dysfunctional families, but, well, I'm calling because I hoped that Dave might be over at your place."

Leah heard a chuckle over the line.

"I'm with you on the dysfunctional bit," Summer commiserated. "That mother of theirs." Bob's mother was also Gerry and Ron Chapman's mother from a previous marriage. "At least Sandy spends time with his half-brother so, hopefully, we won't have a repeat. But, no, Dave's not here."

"Well, I knew it was a longshot..."

"Leah, when did you see him last?"

"Yesterday. Gerry got a little...rough with him. We haven't seen him since last night, and I'm getting worried."

The silence stretched, then Summer finally answered. "I'll keep my eyes out. If he shows up, we'll take care of him, and I'll let you know."

"Thanks, Summer."

"And Leah? If you ever need to talk..."

"I know. Thanks."

The Fairgrounds
Monday, June 28, 1632, 12:45 p.m.

Dave was feeling a lot better after showering in the pool changing rooms. Two nights sleeping rough hadn't done anything for him except make him feel dirty. And cold. And hungry. He wandered over to where the food vendors were clustered and ordered two sausages on a bun, surprised at how quickly they disappeared once he started eating.

He was so focused on his problems that he didn't even notice the old man sitting down on the bench next to him until he heard his name. "Dave? You okay, son?"

A flare of terror ran through him as he turned quickly and saw Millard Barger. "Ah, yes, I'm fine, Mr. Barger."

Barger frowned as he took in Dave's face. "Fine? That's a pretty good shiner you've got there. Trouble at school?"

Dave knew he was blushing, and he couldn't meet Barger's eyes. "Uh, no."

Barger's frown deepened. "Son, that"—he flicked his finger towards Dave's black eye—"doesn't look 'fine.' Looks to me like someone beat on you. If it was another kid at school, well, the best way to deal with it would be to return the favor. If it's someone else..." He let the implication dangle.

Dave felt his blush deepen. "It's, ah, well..."

Barger's eyes flicked to Dave's backpack and rolled blanket, then back to his face. Dave could see him tense, then relax. "Son, as my old sergeant used to say, 'shit happens.'" He held up a hand in negation. "I'm not going to ask, but let me just say that family is important, even if sometimes they're assholes. They're like the army: you're issued your family. Well,"—his eyes twinkled—"at least until you get married."

Dave relaxed a bit and gave him a weak smile. Barger continued, "Thing is, Dave, you can also choose your family." He leaned back and looked around. "That's what 'best friends' are. You build that chosen family over time—years, decades, a lifetime. They're the people who love you for you, and they can become closer than the family you were born into. Sometimes they're blood kin, sometimes not." He shrugged. "My best friend was some type of cousin—third, fourth, who knows? But when he died in Vietnam, I felt like my brother had died. I still miss him every day."

Barger looked back at Dave. "What I'm trying to say, son, is don't be too hasty. But you also need to know that if things are really bad, you have options. Have you ever heard of an 'emancipated minor'?" At Dave's head shake, he continued. "It's a way of cutting yourself off from your family if things are really bad. You need a job and a place to stay, and you have to petition the court for it. It's one of those last-resort things."

Dave was feeling shell-shocked. "Ah, are you suggesting I should do that?"

Barger shook his head. "Hell, no, son! I just want you to know that you have options if they are absolutely necessary. Try and work out what you can, but always remember there are options." He paused for a moment and shook his head. "Almost forgot, I talked with the Vo-Tech admin about you doing translations for me. Turns out they've got a budget for it, so—" He reached into his back pocket and pulled out his wallet, opened it and handed Dave some bills." Here's what I should have been paying you."

"I can't take that!"

"Course you can. You earned it fair and square. And I hope to see you this Friday but, if not, I'll understand." He stood up, leaving the bills on the bench. "Remember what I said, Dave. And if things ever get really bad, you know where I live, and you're welcome to crash for a couple of nights, no questions asked."

Chapman House
6:25 p.m.

Leah was now officially terrified. There had been no news about Dave, and she kept imagining him dead somewhere. Finally, she put down her knife and fork. "Gerald, enough is enough. You need to find Dave, apologize, and bring him home."

Gerry looked up at her. "Apologize? What for?"

Leah glared at him. "For losing your temper. Didn't those anger management classes you took in '87 teach you anything?" Her glare deepened. "Finish your dinner, then go look for Dave. Take Tim with you." Gerry matched her glare, and she hissed at him. "Go. Now. Or I'll call the cops and get them to do it. Or, if you don't want the cops, I could just call Dad."

Gerry blanched, wiped his mouth, and stood up. "Tim. You're with me."

9:50 p.m.

Gerry and Tim returned to their house after a fruitless search. Tim headed upstairs to bed, while Gerry went into the kitchen to face Leah. She looked up at him. "No luck. Some people did see him earlier today over by the fairgrounds, but that's it."

"But some people saw him?"

Gerry nodded. "Yeah. He bought some food, talked with a few people, then left."

Leah breathed out a sigh of relief. "So, he's still alive and in Grantville." She closed her eyes for a moment. "Right, you need to stake out the fairgrounds tomorrow."

"What? I have to work!"

Leah glared at him. "Take a personal day, Gerry. In fact, take as many as you need until Dave is back. And get Tim to check out the other places where he might get food."

A Hilltop South of Murphy's Run
Friday, July 2, 1632, 7:45 p.m.

Happy freaking Birthday to me! Dave thought as he nibbled at the stale bun which was all the food he had left. He had tried to go to the food vendors at the fairgrounds on Tuesday, but had seen his father there and faded. He had managed to get into Stevenson's grocery store and buy some rolls, cheese, and a hard sausage, but he had spotted Tim on the street and took off. He had been hiding in a small copse near the ridge line south of Murphy's Run since then.

What am I going to do, he wondered for probably the fiftieth time. Going home just wasn't an option. He knew his father would beat him black and blue, and his mother wouldn't do a damn thing to stop it. He had seriously thought about going to Mr. Barger's place, but was afraid that Mr. Barger would get in trouble if Dave's father ever found out.

Thinking of Mr. Barger brought their last conversation back to mind. "Shit happens" indeed! Dave snorted, but the memory continued to play out in his mind: "Let me just say that family is important, even if sometimes they're assholes." Dave thought about it, then shrugged. It's not like I have a lot of family in Grantville.

The memory ran on. "Thing is, Dave, you can also choose your family. That's what 'best friends' are. You build that chosen family over time—years, decades, a lifetime. They're the people who love you for you, and they become closer than the family you were born into. Sometimes they're blood kin, sometimes not. My best friend was some type of cousin—third, fourth, who knows?"

Dave thought about that. Cousins? Well, yeah, I have some. The only one I really know at all is Sandy....

Sandy Eckerlin and Dave had gone to school together for years, even though Sandy was a grade ahead. They weren't that close, but it wasn't because they didn't like each other. The problem between them was their grandmother, Ruby Robinson, now Eckerlin, who had first married Dave's grandfather, Augie Chapman, in 1962, then divorced him in 1965 to marry Sandy's grandfather, Lowry Eckerlin. The Chapman and Eckerlin half-siblings didn't get on, probably because of Ruby. In Dave's opinion, his grandmother was a bit of a bitch.

Thoughts of Sandy trailed off as he tried to remember what Mr Barger had said about emaciated—No—emancipated minors. "You need a job and a place to stay, and you have to petition the court for it. It's one of those last-resort things." He felt a tingle run through him. *Sandy has a business. Maybe he can help.*

Eckerlin House
9:35 p.m.

It had taken Dave over an hour to walk to Sandy's house, taking care not to be seen, and he was now watching from the shadows at the rear. *What is going on there?* He watched people moving around in the building behind the house. *It was strange, really.* All the lights were on in both the house and in the manufacturing facility; well, at least in what he could see of it.

Finally, after about fifteen minutes, Dave saw Sandy leaving the manufacturing facility and making his way slowly up to the house. *Damn! He looks totally wiped out!* "Uh, cuz, can I talk with you?"

Sandy frowned and glanced over at him, then did a double-take. "Dave?" Dave nodded as he walked towards Sandy and out of the shadows. "What the..." Sandy squinted, then shook his head and scrunched his nose. "You need a shower. Come on in. You can use mine. I'll find you some clean clothes while we stick those in the wash."

Sandy led Dave into the bottom of the house, through an open area, and into a small but nice bedroom. "The shower's through there." Sandy pointed to a door. "Help yourself, while I find you something to wear. Once you're done, come on up to the kitchen, and I'll have something for you to eat."

Dave mumbled, "Thanks," as he dropped his pack and headed into the bathroom, closing the door behind him and looking around. *How does Sandy rate this?* He took in the compact bathroom before turning on the water and getting out of his dirty clothes. The shower felt wonderful, and he stayed under it until he felt his muscles relax and was clean again.

After toweling dry, he grabbed his dirty clothes and looked into the bedroom, spotting the clothes laid out on the bed. Dropping the dirty clothes on his backpack, he started to get dressed. Too large, he thought as he rolled up the cuffs on the pants and shirt. He smelled something he couldn't identify, but it smelled really good and the enthusiastic sounds coming from his stomach agreed with his nose. Dave let out a sigh. Time to face the music. He left the bedroom and headed to the stairs and up into the kitchen.

When he reached the top, he almost turned around and ran. "Come on up, Dave. Have a seat and something to eat," he heard his Uncle Bob say. He squared his shoulders and came into the kitchen, heading for the only open chair.

As he sat down, he heard the microwave ping. Sandy grabbed a plate out of it, placing it on the table next to him. "Hang on just a sec, and I'll get the rest of it." Sandy walked over to the stove and started to spoon something into a wide, shallow bowl, which he put in front of Dave. "Sorry, it's left-overs. Linguini with an Alfredo sauce, chicken, mushrooms, and asparagus, garlic bread, and there's a bit of Caesar salad left that I can pull out of the refrigerator."

Sandy headed off, and Dave just stared at the food. He could feel tears starting in his eyes as the scent floated behind his brain and, all of a sudden, he felt ravenous. A small plate of salad and a bowl with grated cheese appeared next to him, rapidly followed by a salt shaker and pepper grinder. "Dig in, Dave," he heard his Uncle Bob say, and wasted no time.

Dave was so focused on the food that he barely noticed the young woman who walked in, nodded at Bob, and went over to talk with Sandy. Sandy nodded, went to the freezer, and put something in the microwave. Then he returned to the refrigerator and poured something else in a bowl and started to use a hand beater on it.

Dave was mopping up the last of the sauce with the final piece of garlic bread when he realized that nobody had said anything while he ate. Shit. He popped the last of the garlic bread into his mouth, looked up, and finally noticed what was going on. His uncle Bob sipped a large glass of water as he watched Dave. Sandy and, he presumed, Uncle Bob's new wife each had small glasses of something red.

"Want something to drink, Dave?" Sandy said. "We've got water, iced camomile tea, lemonade, small beer, and red wine. Your choice." He glanced at the microwave. "Dessert in ten or so."

"Uh, lemonade. Thanks, Sandy." Sandy just nodded and went to the fridge.

"I take it," his uncle said, "that your eye comes courtesy of my beloved half-brother."

Dave felt his face heating as he nodded.

He heard his uncle sigh. "Figures. I'd heard he was having a rough time of it since the Ring of Fire, and he's never dealt with stress real well."

Dave saw that the woman's face got sharper as she heard that.

"Dave, I'm pretty sure we met at my wedding, but I don't remember talking with you. Sorry." A smile flitted over her face. "I had other things on my mind. Anyway, I'm Summer. You may as well call me that, especial- ly,"—her eyes flicked to Sandy—"since Sandy does." Turning to Bob, she asked, "Has this happened before?"

Bob nodded. "Not with the kids that I know of. Once, back in '87, with Leah. Gerry snapped and got physical."

Dave could see that Summer's eyes were almost slitted. "What hap- pened?"

Bob leaned back and sipped his water. "The place Gerry was working went bankrupt after Black Monday, so he was out of a job. Leah was taking any shifts she could get, which left Gerry dealing with the kids. Tim was three, and Liz was only a year old. He kept looking for work, but it wasn't until mid-December that he found anything."

"And?" Summer's eyes were definitely slitted now, and her mouth was a thin, tight line.

"He managed to get a job, actually, the one he has now, and he felt that Leah should take over caring for the kids. She didn't agree, and they got into a fight." Dave was staring at Bob. He had never heard anything about this.

"What aren't you telling me, Bob?"

"That fight got physical, and Leah went to hospital with a spiral fracture in her arm." Bob snorted and waved his hand. "It wasn't all one-sided, though. Gerry was off work for a week until the swelling in his balls went down."

Dave's eyes were flicking back and forth between Summer and Bob. Summer was starting to smile. "Really? She kicked him in the nuts?"

Bob snorted. "Kneed him, according to Ron." He waved a hand. "Anyway, with both of them having to go to the hospital, Susan stepped in to take care of the kids. The cops were called, but no charges were laid since Gerry agreed to go to an anger management class, which he did."

Summer toyed with her glass. "So, not a regular reaction, but a pattern when he is stressed?" Bob nodded. "Hmmm, okay. I don't like it, but I can understand it. So..." She leaned back in thought, before her eyes shifted to Dave. "I guess it really comes down to what you want to do, Dave. It's your life, and you need to know that you have some control over it."

Dave was feeling a bit like a deer caught in the headlights. "Ah, well, I, ah... What I really want is to work with my hands. You know, make things. Dad wants me to be a CNA like him, and I just don't want that." He shook his head.

Uncle Bob shifted in his chair. "Is Gerry trying to tell you what you will be?"

Dave nodded. "Yeah, and it's not what I want to be."

Uncle Bob nodded. "He always did try to control everything around him. Just like Mom that way."

"Mr ..." Dave caught himself. "Ah, a friend of mine said that I could become an 'emancipated minor' if I had a job and a place to stay."

Summer nodded. "Yeah, you probably could. It's a drastic step, though. Still..." She turned to Bob with a thoughtful look. "How does Gerry react to threats?"

Bob frowned. "Depends on the threat, but he usually backs down, at least if he doesn't feel cornered."

Summer nodded and smiled. Dave just felt confused.

Sandy started to chuckle while shaking his head. "Leverage?" Summer nodded, and Sandy laughed. He had just opened his mouth to say something when the microwave pinged. "Let me get that." With a crinkled smile he said, "You may as well go ahead, Summer."

Dave was wondering what he was missing as Sandy pulled a dish out of the microwave. Then Summer looked at him and smiled. "How would you like a job, Dave? The pay's lousy, but it comes with a place to stay and three meals a day."

Dave was feeling a bit whipsawed—elated, confused, relieved. "I, uh, well... That is, what would I be doing? I don't know anything about cooking."

Summer laughed. "Neither do I, really. I leave all that up to Sandy and Maestro Amendola. But we do a lot more than cooking; we build a lot of things as well. We've got an all-hands-on-deck project starting on Tuesday. We have to get something designed and built in about two weeks, so the people working on it are going to be going full out, probably twelve to fourteen hours a day, maybe more. And we are going to be short-staffed because of opening the store and all the other stuff we need to get done."

Dave looked interested. "Sounds like fun. So, what are you working on?"

"Building a stove and range that runs on wood and charcoal."

The interest started to drain from Dave's face. "We've already got cast iron stoves. Well, pictures at least, so what's the problem?"

Sandy came back to the table and sat down. "The problem," he said, "is that they won't work for a lot of recipes, both up-time and down-time. Look, did your mother ever make a casserole just using the broiler—that's the upper heating element in one of our stoves."

Dave shrugged. "Sure, but not since we got here and she ran out of canned soup."

Sandy grunted. "I swear, canned condensed soup is the bane of cooking in Grantville! It's, like, in practically every recipe!" With a visible effort, he got himself back on topic. "Anyway, that broiler is a heating element at the top of the oven. How would you build an oven that uses wood that has a top heating element, as well as a lower one?"

Dave opened his mouth, then closed it as he thought about the problem. "Hmm. Maybe put a fire on top?"

Sandy nodded. "That was my first thought. I wanted to put a BBQ on top. Helmut—he's the master blacksmith who runs our operations—told me it wouldn't work because the hottest part of a fire is at the top. He's right, so he's been playing with other options." Sandy shrugged. "I've been so busy getting the store up and running that I haven't been following up on what he thinks will work."

Summer caught Dave's attention. "So, that's what we can offer you, Dave. A chance to work on this project and see if you like what we're doing. The pay sucks, because we can only hire you as an Apprentice 1—basically unskilled labor—but you will get a share of the profits, a place to stay if you want, and three meals a day. Interested?"

Dave took his time and thought about it. It actually sounded kind of cool, and he'd be getting to play with fire, which would probably help him with steam engines. The pay did suck, but the food, if the left-overs were anything to go by, sounded way better than he got at home. "So, is this, like, the only project you guys are working on?"

Sandy rolled his eyes. "As if! Outside of us doing the grand opening of our retail store on Sunday, Gio..., ah, Maestro Amendola wants us to build a mechanical roasting spit to go over a BBQ. I want to figure out if we can build a mechanical stand-mixer or blender. Summer keeps talking about a waffle machine." He shook his head. "It just goes on and on, Dave. I think we're going to have new projects coming out of our butts for the next decade or more."

Dave started to smile. "I'm in." The smile faded. "Well, assuming I can get my parents to agree."

Summer, Bob, and Sandy all smiled. Bob said, "I don't think that will be a problem, Dave."

Sandy stood up, grabbed a plate from the counter and fiddled with it for a moment, lighting a candle. He slid the plate in front of Dave. "Welcome to the company. And Dave? Happy Birthday!"

Dave felt tears running down his cheeks.

Eckerlin House
Saturday, July 3, 1632, 9:05 a.m.

Briinnggg, br ... "Hello?"

Summer leaned back in her chair. "Hi, Leah. It's Summer calling."

"Hi, Summer. Thanks for calling last night and telling me that Dave was there. Is he,"—Leah hesitated—"okay? Is he ready to come home?"

"Okay?" Summer paused herself, then sighed. "Physically, yes. The black eye is healing, but still pretty spectacular. Emotionally? No, he's not. He's feeling betrayed and like he has absolutely no control over his life. If he goes back home right now, he will probably just run again if things get tense and, if he does, I doubt he will come here."

Summer could hear a stifled sob.

"Well, I, ah. Oh, fuck it! I am going to kill Gerry for this!"

Summer chuckled. "No reason to kill him, when you can make him suffer. Maybe even teach him a lesson." The warmth left her voice. "Bob told me about '87, including what you did to him then. I think that something similar is in order."

"What did you have in mind? I'm not sure I'm up to busting his balls again."

Summer laughed at that. "Tempting, but no. What I'm thinking of is having Dave come to work for us. I offered him a job last night on a temporary basis for the next couple of weeks, but it could become permanent if he likes the work. He gets minimal pay, profit sharing, and room and board. He accepted, but he's not old enough to sign an employment contract."

This time the silence lasted longer. "Ah, how does that bust Gerry's balls?"

"It gives Dave everything he needs to get emancipated minor status if Gerry gets out of line again." Summer heard Leah's sudden intake of breath. "No, Dave doesn't want to sever ties with his family. But he really, really needs to feel in control of his life, and this will let him do that." Summer sniggered. "Well, at least until he finds out about our den mother who makes sure the apprentices go to school and do their homework."

Leah's hysterical laughter came crackling over the line. "Oh, my! That will be a surprise." The line went silent again. "Fine, it sounds like it will be good for him. I'll sign his employment contract, and if Gerry pushes it, he'll find out I still know how to use my knees. You send me a copy, and I'll sign it while Gerry is still at work."

Summer was smiling. "It should be delivered in about forty-five minutes. Thanks, Leah."

Chapman House
7:05 p.m.

Gerry walked into the house after his first shift in almost a week. It fucking had to be a twelve-hour one, too! "I'm home! Is dinner ready? I'm starving!"

"In the kitchen."

Gerry walked back to the kitchen and sat down, looking around. "Where are the kids?"

Leah filled a bowl and gave it to him. "Liz and Tim are out with friends."

Gerry frowned. "And Dave? I thought he would be home by now."

Leah sat down and looked Gerry in the eyes. "He's not coming home for several weeks. He has a job and will be staying with Summer at her manufactory."

Gerry scowled. "What?!? How in the hell did that happen?"

Leah's eyes narrowed. "He ran away because of you. I'm not sure how he ended up at Bob and Summer's place, but he did. And he needs time to feel that he has some control over his life." She leaned forward, eyes fully slitted. "And you still have to apologize to him, which you will do tomorrow afternoon. Understand?"

Gerry gulped, then waved a hand. "Fine." He took a spoon of stew and chewed it, then swallowed. "So what's this job he has?" Gerry's mind hiccuped. "Wait a minute, he's only twelve. He can't get a job without my approval, and I sure as hell didn't give it!"

Leah just shook her head. "Gerry, sometimes I think you are as dumb as a box of rocks! The law says he can't get a job without parental approval. I signed the contract earlier today."

Gerry felt a rush of anger. How DARE she sign something like that without even talking with him! He reined in his anger. "Do you have a copy of this contract?"

Leah handed him a piece of paper, which he took and started to read. "What?!? Oh, no fucking way! Why in the HELL would you sign this?"

Leah's eyes narrowed again. "Because Dave wanted it. And Gerry, you are not going to bugger this up, or you will regret it for the small amount of time you have left on this earth!"

Summer's Kitchen Store
Sunday, July 4, 1632, 1:30 p.m.

Dave had gained a new appreciation the day before for just how hard cooking could be when you were in the seventeenth century. After an early breakfast, he had been given a quick tour of the facility by Sandy, shown his bunk, and then set to what he was told was the fate of unskilled apprentices: grinding grain into flour using a quern. Two hours and twenty pounds of flour later, he was set to cutting up mushrooms while others made pasta. By the time lunch came, he was both exhausted and ravenous.

Lunch was an eye-opener: bits of chicken, spinach, mushrooms, carrots and spinach fried in bacon fat and olive oil with spaghetti, served with garlic bread. Unfortunately, it was over too soon, and Dave was stuck back on the quern for another two hours and twenty pounds, followed by slicing mushrooms and, for a change, asparagus.

A reprieve, in the form of helping with a delivery to the store, came around four in the afternoon, then back for dinner at seven and a final briefing on the grand opening. Who would have thought that a cooking and kitchenware business would be run like a military unit? Still, it did sound like a major production, especially since they were combining the opening with a Pay What You Can BBQ, serving pasta and sauce, lasagna, and wraps containing chicken and vegetables.

Today had started early as well. After breakfast, Dave had gone with several people to pick up food that had already been prepared and stored in several places, then back to the store. As he loaded the containers into their small cart, he marveled at the dishes themselves. Huh! Seventeenth-century food storage. Who would have thought it could be made out of pottery? I wonder if that's why Sandy calls it Töpferware. Then it was back to the store to unload for a quick lunch before the parade ended.

Dave had just finished bringing out another container of skewers—Sandy called it Chicken on a Stick—when he spotted his family coming towards them. Oh, fuck. He saw the expression on his father's face. "Sandy," he said quietly as he put the container on a table, "my dad's coming, and he looks pissed."

Sandy glanced up from the BBQ and spotted Gerry, Leah, Tim, and Liz. "Right. Head back into the store and help out with the pasta sales. I'll handle this. Dad and Summer are around if I need backup."

"Thanks." Dave felt like a coward leaving Sandy, but it was better than having a public confrontation with his father. He didn't think his father would hit him in public, but he didn't want to put that to the test. As he wove his way through the increasingly crowded store, he could see why Sandy wanted him to help with the pasta sales. The entire cheese, pasta, and condiments station was swamped. He stepped behind the station and asked Adolph, the journeyman in charge, what he needed.

"Dank, Dave. Wir brauchen mehr pasta. In back."

Dave nodded and went to the stacks of Töpferware, looking for white pieces of cloth attached to the lids. Yesterday, Dave had asked Sandy about that and been told that it was the simplest way to label contents. They had even designed the dishes so that they had a slot on one of the short edges of the lid for that very purpose. Dave scanned the stacks, then grabbed two containers and brought them back, picked up several empty ones, and headed back for more.

After he dropped off the second set of pasta, Adolph told him, "Ernst braucht mehr chicken on a stick, und noch zwei, two, Lasagnen." Back Dave went, grabbing two containers of skewers and taking them outside, returning with empties. A second trip with two containers of lasagna followed, and Dave took a breather. Those suckers are heavy. Across the road, he could see Sandy talking with his parents while Tim and Liz looked on, eating wraps.

"Dave?" Ernst said as he paused between orders. "Mehr pasta und sauce, bitte." Dave nodded and headed back inside, grabbing two containers of pasta, while a second trip brought two containers of sauce. Good thing the sauce is in these half-sized containers. He put them on a table behind the BBQ. Glancing at the BBQ, he saw that Ernst was already halfway through the second container of skewers. He took the empties inside and brought two more containers of skewers out front.

He had just put the new containers down when he spotted Sandy and his family coming over. He caught Sandy's eye and cocked his head. Sandy nodded, smiled, and waved him over. That smile defused some of Dave's anxiety, as did the matching smile on his mother's face. Still nervous, he came out from behind the BBQ and walked over to them. "Dad. Mom. Ah, good to see you."

"Dave," his mother swept him into a hug, then released him. "I'm really glad to see you're okay. You scared us all." She looked over at his father. "Gerry?"

Dave's father looked, well, Dave wasn't sure what he looked like. "Uh, Davey...Sorry, Dave. I, ah, want to apologize for last Saturday. I had a really bad day and just wasn't myself and things, well, got out of hand. I'm sorry about that." Gerry shook himself, then continued. "So, you've got a job. I hope you enjoy it." Gerry hooked a thumb at Sandy. "I tried to renegotiate with your cheapskate cousin, but he won't budge."

His mother rolled her eyes, then said, "Dave, I hope you will consider coming home again, at least for visits. I know that won't be likely for at least a couple of weeks—Summer tells me you've got an all-hands-on-deck project—but, after that? Please come."

Dave could see the pleading in his mother's eyes. "Okay, Mom. I'll see what I can do and when."

His mother hugged him again, grabbed his father, and they walked off, followed by a listless Liz. Sandy had already returned to the BBQ, leaving Dave and Tim alone.

"Way to go, little bro!" Tim said with a smile. "Now I've got the bedroom to myself and you'll escape the bedpans." The smile slipped. "Dave, I've gotta warn you—Sandy is one manipulative shit, so watch out for him. He twisted Dad up like Hulk Hogan used to slam people. Dad didn't know how to deal with any of it and probably won't figure it out for a month, if then." The smile returned. "I'm going to grab some of that pasta, but I'll see you around."

Summer's Kitchen Workshop
8:45 p.m.

Dave leaned back and sipped his lemonade, relaxing in the twilight. What a day! He remembered the crush at the opening and the emotionally charged scene with his family. *I still can't believe Dad apologized, but I'm glad he did.* Another sip as he thought about how the rest of the day had gone. They had had to close down the BBQ just after four because they had run out of food, but no one really seemed to mind.

Dave's eyes flicked towards where Summer, Sandy, Maestro Amendola, and Master Förster were sitting, their faces wreathed in big smiles. *Looks like the day was a success financially as well, from the shit-eating grins they're wearing.* Slowly, he started to smile. *I shouldn't be surprised. By two-thirty, we were selling entire lasagnas and containers of pasta and sauce.* He saw Sandy say something, then stand up and move towards him.

"All ready for tomorrow, Dave?"

Dave narrowed his eyes. "I thought we had tomorrow off? You know, on account of us working like fourteen, fifteen hours for the past couple of days."

Sandy snorted. "Yeah, well, that was before we got orders for like a hundred pounds of fresh pasta. And fifty pounds of sauce. Maestro Amendola will be working a lot of people tomorrow to get that ready. He'll be up at four-thirty in the morning, but"—Sandy shrugged—"that won't involve you, so you can sleep until six-thirty or so."

"Really?" Dave relaxed. "That's good. So, what do you have me doing tomorrow?"

Sandy nodded. "We've got a design meeting tomorrow afternoon on the new stoves. You, me, Joe, Maestro Amendola, Master Förster, and someone he just hired; maybe a few others. Despite the orders, we're all off kitchen duty."

Dave breathed a sigh of relief. "Good. I thought my shoulder would fall off after using that quern for a couple of hours!" He squinted his eyes and looked at Sandy. "You don't have me doing that in the morning, do you?"

Sandy shook his head and, Dave thought, tried to project an air of innocence. "Kitchen duty in the morning, Dave? No, no, no! After all," he said with a shark-like grin, "we can't interfere with your schooling!"

Dave stared at him in horror. "What?!? School?!?!?"

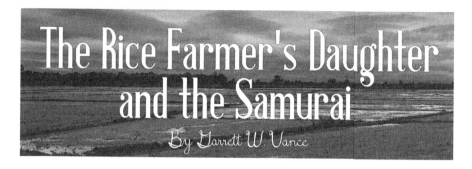

The Rice Farmer's Daughter And The Samurai

Garrett W. Vance

Nishioka House, Nihonmachi, Phnom Penh, Kingdom of Khmer, Indochina
1635

The stoic people of Nihonmachi worked mostly in silence as they went about the grim task of cleaning up after a brief, brutal pitched battle. A relatively small number of Ishida's samurai had eradicated a larger, but undisciplined, band of river pirates while suffering only a few minor wounds themselves. The samurai now worked in pairs, picking up the blood-soaked, stinking corpses of their foes and loading them on the wagons that would haul them away for burning in the charnel grounds beyond the city.

Ishida, influential businessman, community leader, and the mercenary warrior troop's commander, looked on approvingly, proud of how well his men had acquitted themselves in the fierce fray. Imagine what they could do with those guns from the future! The thought brought a rare smile to his usually stern face. *We could liberate Ayutthaya from the usurper king with weapons like that. The winds of opportunity bear us to the far west where they are made and we will learn how to use them, then the winds of vengeance will bear us back to the east....*

Ishida turned to his next order of business. He needed to ensure the safety of the Nishiokas' little girl, four-year-old Hana, who had been very fortunately absent during the attack, under the care of the very capable Tanaka daughters. He knew just the promising young warrior to manage that.

"Hachisuka! Go to the Tanaka home and bear word to their eldest daughter, Junko, that there was a disturbance here, and that all are safe. Just say it was a break-in and that we are on watch for any other robbers in the area tonight. We don't want to alarm her. We shall let her mother do that." It was common knowledge in Nihonmachi that if you wanted everyone to know something, just tell Mrs. Tanaka—a lovely person, but also an inveterate gossip.

"Instruct Junko to simply tell little Hana that her parents have asked her to stay there tonight because they are busy preparing for the trip. Mrs. Tanaka has agreed to all of this. Station yourself at their door until I send relief, and admit no strangers. Refer them to me instead. If any resist, you know what to do!"

"*Hai!*" The handsome young warrior was just nineteen years of age, but already well-trained by Ishida and his troop's more experienced samurai. He bowed to his master, then turned to hurry off to his duty.

* * *

Unexpectedly, Sano, their resident healer, stepped into his path.

"Young sir, please. Your clothes are all covered in blood! We don't want poor little Hana to know what happened, nor frighten the Tanaka children, so you need to change!"

Hachisuka nodded his understanding, then looked over to Ishida for instruction.

"Do what she says," he told him.

"Wait in the laundry room under the house." Sano gave orders him as if she were just as much his commander as Ishida was. The formidable woman always had Ishida's ear, in part because she had saved the lives of so many of Ishida's wounded over the years. So said the men who had been with him in Ayutthaya, fighting the Burmese beside the Siamese forces. Ishida always made it clear to his men to obey her implicitly when undergoing her treatments, which was probably unnecessary considering her no-nonsense demeanor—all the samurai respected Sano, if they knew what was good for them.

Hachisuka bowed politely to her and walked under the house, which was pleasantly cool in the shade. He looked at the two-dozen-odd river pirate corpses that Nishioka's wife Momo had slain with her husband's *wakizashi*. Hachisuka admired the woman's courage and ability greatly. Her husband had taught her well. He had never had the chance to study under Nishioka, of whom the older men spoke reverently. Hachisuka had been brought by Ishida's recruiter in Japan directly to Phnom Penh well after Nishioka had retired from service. Hachisuka had to smile at Nishioka's "just a humble boatman" bit. Nishioka Yoriaki was a legend among his peers.

Being young, bored, and seeking glory over a humdrum life in rural Aichi province in Japan, Hachisuka had eagerly accepted Ishida's offer and sailed away to adventure. He hadn't been disappointed. Today wasn't his first real fight, but it had certainly been the most intense! It was amazing to him that a samurai of Nishioka's station would give it all up to marry a Kirishitan girl and settle down to be a *bento* vendor. When he had asked his older comrades about it, they just smiled and told him, "It seems you have never met his wife Momo."

Well, he had seen her, and she was indeed a woman of great grace and beauty—and now, bravery and the reputation of being a fierce, skillful fighter had been added to her list of admirable qualities. Still, Hachisuka, at nineteen years of age, couldn't imagine any girl, no matter how pretty she was, drawing him away from the thrill of the warrior way.

In the small, brick-walled laundry room, Hachisuka leaned against the wooden table to wait. To his surprise, a pile of clothes landed on the table with a soft thump, making him jump. He turned and looked up to see Sano's round face looking down at him through a square hatchway in the washroom floor above him.

"Ha! Looks like I got the drop on you, samurai!"

Hachisuka didn't bristle as some young men might have. He rather liked old Sano; she had patched him up a few times, and her caustic wit was just part and parcel with her course of medicines. He just laughed and looked up to meet her grin with one of his own.

"Those are Nishioka Yoriaki's old samurai clothes," she said. "I don't think he will mind if you borrow them. After all, he no longer wears them! I'm a bit surprised he even kept them after his early retirement." Hachisuka saw her eyes unfocus for just an instant as if she were having an important thought. She cocked her head as if filing something away in her mind, then said, "Anyway, I thought they would be more befitting of a young warrior of good standing like yourself than those frumpy old rags he wears out boating."

"Thank you, Sano-san." He answered with a polite bow, awkwardly trying to direct it at Sano, standing above his head.

Sano just laughed at his attempt. "Get moving!" She let the hatch door slam shut with a loud bang that made him jump again, glad that she hadn't been able to see him do it.

Nishioka's clothing was of a far more expensive make than he himself could afford, cut in the classic style of their homeland, but crafted from fine Siamese silk. Hachisuka wrapped his own modest attire up, bloodstains and all, and tied it into a bundle with a bit of line he cut from a roll of cord left out on the table. Feeling quite the dandy in his borrowed attire, he made a point of not strutting and showing it off to the other samurai who were still busy loading bodies on wagons. Not wishing for Ishida to change his mind and give him that grisly and foul-smelling duty over the much preferable one he had drawn, he made a quick beeline for the gate and hurried up the dusty street to the Tanakas' home.

The Tanakas lived about halfway between the Nishioka house and the town's center where Ishida and Sano both had homes. He himself lived in a barracks a bit over a mile beyond the town's central square. His quarters were spartan, but more than enough for an up-and-coming warrior such as himself. The Tanaka home was on a narrower side street called "Rice Road" that ran a few hundred yards away from the main road, divided from both it and the downtown by swaths of orchards. A row of simple, well-built homes lined it, rice paddies behind them spreading out far and wide—all the way out to the Mekong River several miles distant.

Young Hachisuka arrived at the Tanaka home's bamboo front gate and announced himself politely.

"Tanaka family! I am Hachisuka, sent by Ishida-san with news!" He waited for a few moments, hearing a rustle of activity coming from inside the house. Shortly after, the door opened and a young woman shyly leaned out of it, her dark eyes blinking in the afternoon glare.

"I am Tanaka Junko, eldest daughter. What news do you bring, samurai?" she called back in a clear, alto voice, her tone impeccably formal.

Hachisuka took a moment to answer, a bit stunned by the young woman's beauty. He found his own voice and attempted to make it sound sufficiently commanding.

"There has been a disturbance at the Nishioka house. All is well now," Hachisuka announced.

"What disturbance?" she asked, concerned for her friends.

"A break-in." Hachisuka carefully followed Ishida's script. "The matter has been resolved, but we are on alert in case there is more trouble."

"Are the Nishiokas all right?"

"Yes, the Nishiokas are quite safe. They are busy with the move and they wish you to keep their daughter Hana with you tonight. Your mother is in agreement, and will return to you later."

A small face appeared beside Junko's gracefully curved hip, and stared at the young samurai with a child's guileless curiosity. Hana. Junko gently reached down and pushed the child back inside. Hana's face was immediately replaced by another at shoulder height, obviously a sister of Junko, a year or two younger. Hachisuka smiled, amused by the children's interest, then resumed his official demeanor, an act made surprisingly difficult by his urge to stare into Junko's lovely eyes.

"Meanwhile, I will stay here and keep watch." He followed this with a curt bow, and turned back to the street to begin his duties.

* * *

Junko stared at the young samurai's muscular back long enough that her fifteen-year-old sister Tamiko snickered. "Kawaii, neh? He's cute, isn't he?" she teased Junko, who had recently turned eighteen.

"*Shizuka!* Shush!" Junko ordered her as she pulled the door shut, but not before taking one last look at their protector. He is cute, isn't he? She mused to herself, being sure to hide the blush that was spreading across her face from the siblings gathered behind her.

She reached down to pick up Hana. "Come with me Hana-chan, your parents are busy and you will stay with us tonight. You can help us make dinner!"

Hana nodded agreeably, but looked past her beloved babysitter to the door. She wondered what her mother and father were doing, but staying with the Tanakas was a fairly regular occurrence. Momma Tanaka always told her, "You are here to give your poor mother a rest!" Hana loved having a bunch of big brothers and sisters to play with, so for now she contented herself with helping Junko and Tamiko in the kitchen, always an amusing diversion.

* * *

"Do you think he's hungry?" Tamiko slid the rice-paper window screen open a narrow crack to steal a peek at the young samurai. He stood straight as an arrow in front of the gate, scanning Rice Road with a stern glare as if daring any lurking interlopers to come forth and do battle. Tamiko smirked a little. *Just who was going to assault the Tanaka home anyway? Robbers come to steal our hidden gold? They would be sorely disappointed.*

Junko walked over and shoved the screen closed, almost catching the tip of her younger sister's nose, which would have served her right for spying.

"Of course he's hungry! All young men are hungry, all of the time," Junko told her matter-of-factly. "That is why we are going to take him this *bento* for dinner. Here, you carry the drinking water."

Junko took a moment to push a pickled plum into just the right spot in one of the box's compartments. The attractive arrangement of food completed, she clicked the dark green laminated lid into place.

Tamiko giggled, as was her frequent custom. "That is a fine-looking *bento* you have made for the brave young samurai at our gate," she told her sister insincerely. "Perhaps he will be so impressed by your cooking he will ask to marry you, the way Nishioka Yoriaki did Momo-san!"

Before she picked up the boxed meal, Junko spared a moment to fix on Tamiko the cold, superior glare she reserved for impertinent siblings. But as she walked toward the front door, she thought to herself that it *was* a rather fine *bento*, and she *did* hope their guardian would like it.

"Maybe he will give up being a samurai so that after you are wed you can make food for him to sell from a boat in Grantville! Assuming they have boats, of course," Tamiko mused in a dreamy, teasing tone.

"*Shizuka shinasai mou!* That's enough out of you already!" Junko hissed at her in a tone that would brook no further dissension. Tamiko placed her hand over her lips in mock surrender and followed her, carrying the water bucket, ladle, and a wooden cup.

The younger children knew there was no chance of them being invited on this mission of mercy, so they just watched silently. Little Hana, however, was waiting in the stone-floored *genkan* entryway for them, with her tiny *geta* wooden sandals already on her feet.

Junko sighed. "Hana, I think it's best you stay inside with the other children." The patient babysitter addressed her charge in the kind of gentle tones that usually worked on the child.

"*Ikitai.* I want to go with you," Hana stated matter-of-factly, her small face plainly determined. Junko thought that the child usually looked more like her mild-mannered father, but this was her mother Momo's calm but indisputable resolve in full view now, a facet of her older friend that she very much admired. Like mother, like daughter!

"But Hana, it will be getting dark soon!" Junko tried to reason with her.

"I'm not afraid!"

"Of course you aren't, but Hana—" Junko started to say, but Hana quickly interrupted.

"*Ikitai-iiii!* I want to go with youuu!" Hana's voice took on an obstinate, keening quality that Junko knew would lead to a tantrum if she didn't yield to the child's demands.

"Oh, very well then! But I will be telling your mother about your obstinate behavior," Junko scolded her, exasperated, but also trying not to laugh at little Hana's fierce posturing.

"Here, Hana, help me by carrying the ladle," Tamiko told the child. Hana's grim expression instantly changed to an eager desire to be of service. Tamiko was herself a clever babysitter in the making. She had learned by assisting Junko, three years her elder, from the time she was old enough to make the switch from "baby" to sitter.

"*Hai!*" Hana replied proudly, placing the long ladle over her small shoulder as if she were carrying a *naginata* blade staff.

Junko slipped into her *geta* wooden sandals, then slid open the front door. Hachisuka heard the sound and turned quickly, his hand instinctively reaching for the hilt of his *katana*. This hyper-alert behavior almost made Junko laugh aloud, but she was able to smother it, although she heard a snort emanate from Tamiko behind her.

"We are bringing you dinner, Hachisuka-san!" Junko called out to him.

"We mean you no harm!" Tamiko added, earning her a hiss of warning from Junko.

Hana marched ahead of them with a very fierce look on her face, now brandishing the ladle as if she would defend her older friends with it if the samurai decided to attack. She was soon joined by the Tanakas' dog Kaki, who had awoken from his nap in the cool shade beneath the house. The sturdy little ring-tailed, pointy-eared dog, who had been named for the red-orange persimmon fruit his coat's colors resembled, moved protectively in front of the small child he had come to adore, a low growl of warning rumbling in his throat. Poor Hachisuka looked a bit nonplussed as the procession drew near and had the good sense to raise his hands in surrender.

Junko sighed, and hurried to step in front of her erstwhile protectors, ready to defend their worried-looking guardian from them.

"Kaki! *Yamenasai!* Knock it off!" she ordered the fearless little dog. Kaki stopped growling but stayed glued to Hana's side, his bright, burnt-orange eyes never leaving the hapless samurai.

"I apologize for the rudeness of my assistants," Junko told him, sparing a withering glance at her companions who simply blinked back with expressions innocent of all wrongdoing. "We have brought you a *bento* for your dinner." She lifted the dark green box up to him with both hands while bowing her head respectfully.

"Oh! Well, I shouldn't, err, you shouldn't have, err—" Hachisuka, who was not accustomed to dealing with attractive young women, hesitated in confusion, his face flushing.

Tamiko sighed and told him bluntly, "Just take it, samurai. She worked so hard on it for you!" Her eyes rolled with impatience at the young fellow's thickness. Tamiko would never have taken such an impudent tone with an older samurai, but this one was just a kid about Junko's age.

Junko's eyes widened with embarrassment, but the young warrior did snap out of his stupor.

"*Hai! Doumo!* Of course. Thank you." Hachisuka reached out to take the proffered box, his fingers accidentally brushing Junko's as their eyes locked for a moment. Now both of them flushed, which caused Tamiko to hide another snicker behind her hand.

Tamiko, taking pity on the obviously dumbstruck older teens, broke the spell by asking in honeyed tones, "Hachisuka-san, would you care for some water?"

The young samurai blinked, then nodded as he gingerly took the *bento* box, which Junko released into his hands with a mortified expression.

"Here, come sit on the stone bench. My father put it there for us to rest on." With a flamboyant flourish, Tamiko motioned to the large slab of naturally flat stone near the gate, enjoying every second of the teen drama unfolding before her mischievous fifteen-year-old eyes.

"Hana, the ladle, please." Tamiko reached down toward the child, who had to pause a moment to decide whether to give up her weapon or not, but the desire to display her impeccable good manners to her elders won out, and she held it up to Tamiko with an angelic smile.

"*Douzou!* Here you are." Hana spoke in a sweet, generous tone that made it hard to believe she had been so fierce just a short time before. Kaki sat down directly in front of the samurai and stared at him as he opened the box. Kaki was still suspicious, but also thought there might be a treat in it for him.

"Kaki!" Junko scolded the little dog, finally finding her voice again.

Hachisuka picked up the pointed-tip, orange-colored *hashi* chopsticks that lay on top of the still steaming rice, and deftly picked up one of the small pork *dango* meatballs from their square enclosure. He caught the dog's watchful eye and flicked it toward him. Kaki snapped it out of the air with a bright flash of sharp teeth, then gulped it down immediately.

Junko shook her head in disapproval. "It is very kind of you to share, Hachisuka-san, but there is no need to spoil Kaki. He is quite well fed," she informed him in a cool tone, unhappy that one of the meatballs she had specially made to please him had gone to their thoroughly spoiled and rather rotund dog.

Hachisuka's smile made both of the older girls' hearts skip a beat, while Hana just stared at him with unabashed curiosity. "I assure you, kind ladies, that it was a selfish gesture, meant only to ensure that I remain in the good graces of this fearsome beast!"

This made everyone laugh, but Hana grabbed Kaki in a bear hug. "Kaki is *not* a beast! He is my very good friend!" Kaki just held still, knowing it was best not to resist his beloved small person's firm demonstrations of affection, and simply smiled his best dog smile, hoping to win another meatball.

Hachisuka felt shy at being observed, but it soon became plain that his benefactors were determined to watch him eat every bite. The eldest, Junko, in particular seemed to take a keen interest in his preferences. He stole a glance at her occasionally as he made a point of chewing each morsel with gusto. It truly was delicious, and Junko was very, very pretty. After polishing off the last lump of rice he ate the sour *umeboshi* plum pickle, making a show of it by sucking in his cheeks, pursing his lips, and blowing out a low whistle, which made the gathered girls all laugh.

Hachisuka then located the meatball he had been saving and gave it to Kaki, this time handing it directly to him. The little orange-furred dog took it politely from his fingers with nary a nip and chewed on it happily while Hachisuka took the liberty of scratching him behind the ears. Kaki closed his eyes and licked his chops, enjoying the attention.

"It looks like you have made a friend," Junko told him with an admiring look. "He usually doesn't get close to strangers."

"Then perhaps I am not a stranger anymore." Hachisuka's own shyness abated enough to actually converse with his new female acquaintances. "That was a delicious *bento*. I thank you all very much." He placed the now empty box down on the stone bench behind him.

"Well, you certainly did polish it all off," Tamiko remarked, earning her a sharp elbow in the side from Junko.

"I hope it was enjoyable," Junko said with a humble bow, the question implicit.

"Very," he reassured her, patting his full belly with satisfaction.

Now that Hachisuka was finished with his meal and standing up, Hana, who had been staring at him studiously, decided that she liked him. After all, he was a samurai, just like her father used to be. She released the dog from her iron grip to go stand in front of the young warrior. She then lifted her arms up at him and issued a command.

"*Daite!* Pick me up!"

"*Eh?* What?" Hachisuka hesitated, looking down skeptically at Hana, then up at her babysitters imploringly.

"You better do it, samurai," Tamiko told him without any sympathy at all.

Junko laughed, and for once agreed with her younger sister. "Yes, I think you had better do as she says! If you know what's good for you." Both sisters laughed then, and Hachisuka blew out an exasperated breath.

"*Hai-hai.* Understood," he said, giving into little Hana's demands. He reached down, pondering a moment on how exactly to lift the expectant child, then gripped her firmly under each arm and lifted her so that he was holding her out in front of him at arm's length, which made Junko and Tamiko both snort, then laugh loudly at their brave guardian's discomfiture when faced with a demanding four-year-old.

"*Baka!* Idiot!" Tamiko told him between laughs. "She's *not* a cat." This pithy observation made Junko double over in laughter, quite unable to control herself.

Hana looked a bit confused at all the fuss, and began to impatiently move her arms up and down toward the reluctant samurai.

"*Mou, chantou daitei, Onii-chan.* Go on and hold me right, older brother."

Junko took a deep breath and brought herself under control, now embarrassed that she had laughed so hard at the young warrior, suddenly fearing he might take it personally and come to dislike her.

"Here," she said in measured tones. "Bring her to your chest." Junko stepped toward them and gently pushed Hana forward. Hachisuka quickly understood and brought the child, now beaming happily at all the attention, to his chest and held her there. Junko didn't let go of Hana until she was sure that Hachisuka held her firmly, then lingered, both of them holding the child between them for a long moment, giving Tamiko another opportunity to snicker loudly at the sight.

"What a lovely family you would make!" She opined in dulcet tones. Her sister and Hachisuka both blushed hotly and Hana laughed happily as she grabbed her big new friend by the nose.

"*Suki.* I like you." she announced, making Hachisuka smile despite his consternation.

"I like *you*, too, Hana-chan," he replied in a silly nasal tone that made Hana squeal with delight, but his eyes rested on Junko's face as he said it, just long enough that her eyes widened and another round of snickers came bursting forth from Tamiko.

Satisfied, Hana released the good-natured victim of her affections and was transferred to Junko.

Hachisuka attempted to reclaim his soldierly composure. He gave the girls a very polite bow and thanked them again for the dinner.

Junko returned the bow with a somewhat deeper one than the situation warranted, and told him "Please let us know if you need anything. We will return to the house now." Then she turned and marched up the path to the door without looking back, with Hana hanging over her shoulder waving. Tamiko followed along, frequently looking back at their guardian with a cheerful grin, thoroughly enjoying the discomfiture of her moonstruck elders.

At the doorway Junko handed Hana off to Tamiko and ushered them inside ahead of her. It was then that she realized someone was missing. She looked back to see Kaki standing next to Hachisuka, who had returned to his solemn duties, posting himself just outside the front gate. Junko started to call him in, but then thought to herself, *Well, it would seem Kaki approves of him.* Then she craned her neck to catch one more look at Hachisuka's strong, broad back. *I suppose I do, too.* She smiled as she closed the door, knowing that they were safe under two sets of watchful eyes.

* * *

It was getting near sunset. Junko lit the lantern that she would hang on the post beside the gate for their guardsman and her parents, who she thought might be coming home late. She had come to grow curious about the nature of the disturbance at the Nishioka house and intended to get some answers.

Tamiko was eyeing her with a pouty expression, under strict orders to remain inside with Hana and the other children. She had engaged them in a game of *karuta* cards, spread out across the main room's supple tatami rice mat floor. They were playing a simple "remember and match" set of rules that even little Hana could compete in. Tamiko's job was to distract their young charge so Junko could slip out to find out what had actually happened that had all the adults so occupied. Tamiko's curiosity was also piqued, so she didn't resist her elder sister's commands, expecting a full report when Junko returned.

Tamiko looked up to see Junko heading for the genkan, making sure she blocked the view from the always curious Hana, who was distracted by her search for the still-hidden card that matched the one she had just turned over. Tamiko made a kissy-kissy face at her sensitive sibling, and Junko scowled back before she slipped out the door.

Holding the lamp before her, she walked through late afternoon shadows down the flagstone path to the gate. Hachisuka turned from his vigil and bowed to her with a slight smile. Junko returned both with what she hoped was charm and grace.

"Tanaka-san," he greeted her in his pleasant baritone voice.

"Hachisuka-san." She stepped past him with a duck of her head to hang the lantern on its accustomed nail in the post beside the gate.

"Ah. *Doumou*. Oh, thanks." he told her. He had not moved aside to give her more space and they were very near each other, just inches apart. This made Junko feel embarrassed for a moment, but then she realized that she found his proximity—what? Comforting? It was not unpleasant, in any case. After lingering there for a moment longer than she should have, Junko turned to take a step back up the path but stopped at the sight of a neatly tied cloth bundle lying in the deepening shadows.

"What are those?" Junko stepped toward the little pile.

"Oh, just my laundry."

But Junko thought his nonchalant tone held a ring of some other, deeper emotion.

"Well, I'm going to do some laundry later tonight, so I will just add yours." She quickly bent over and picked up the bundle before Hachisuka could say or do anything to stop her.

"I wash the younger one's clothes all the time, a little extra is no bother," she told him, eager to do something to thank the earnest young samurai for standing his patient watch. But watch for what danger? Robbers? It occurred to her then that she still had questions to ask. That was when she noticed that Hachisuka looked oddly alarmed, and his eyes were darting down to the bundle she held. She followed his gaze to see that the clothing was splattered with a dark red, flaking substance. Dried blood.

"*Ara!* Oh my!" she gasped, but to her credit she didn't drop them. She looked up at him as he shrugged his shoulders in a gesture of helplessness.

"I am very sorry. That isn't pleasant. Just drop them back down there. You don't need to wash them for me." His face looked pale under the lantern's glow now that darkness was drawing near.

Junko took a deep breath and composed herself. "It's all right. I will take care of it for you, and I won't let the little ones see. Just a moment." She turned and hurried across the yard carrying the bloody bundle to the laundry room built into the house's side.

Only a dim light seeped into the laundry room from the open door, but she didn't need much to navigate this familiar space. She untied the bundle then dropped Hachisuka's clothes in a bucket of cold water that sat on the stone floor beside the wash basin. She knew that cold water helped dissolve bloodstains, thanks to the cuts and scrapes her siblings came crying home with after playing too roughly. She would get them out and try not to think about their grisly origins. In any case, no one would find them here tonight, and she would have them cleaned before morning.

She took a moment to calm herself, her own pulse pumping hard. Something bad had happened at the Nishioka home. There had been bloodshed, and now she desperately wanted to know that her friends were actually safe! Taking a deep breath and letting it out with a whoosh, she walked quickly back across the yard and stood in front of the samurai, arms crossed over her blue summer kimono.

The samurai had now retreated to a position in the shadows just at the edge of the lantern's glow.

"What happened?"

"There was a disturbance."

"Yes, obviously. What kind of 'disturbance,' exactly? A violent one, judging by your blood-soaked clothing." Junko's demeanor had changed from shy and possibly moonstruck to the curt, commanding tones she needed to control her sometimes-unruly siblings when she was in charge while her parents worked hard on the rice farm.

Hachisuka squirmed. "Ishida told me only to tell you that much."

"Yes, and I am telling you to tell me what really happened! The Nishiokas are my dear friends, as good as family, and I have to know right now that they are actually safe!" She took a menacing step toward him, the lantern light casting fire on her dark eyes. Hachisuka had met death face to face in combat many times for one so young, and had triumphed, yet now he took a step backward in the face of a kind of force he had little experience with.

Junko matched that step, leaning into him, her clenched fists now on her hips, her very pretty face as fierce as any foe he had ever encountered, her utterly fascinating-to-behold chest rising and falling rapidly as her temper grew. Weighing his options for a moment, the only sensible course of action for the flummoxed young samurai was to give her what she wanted. After all, he could certainly understand her concern. Hachisuka let out a long sigh, and spread his hands wide to signal his compliance.

"Perhaps you had best sit down..."

* * *

Hachisuka finished up the tale of the day's violence and its aftermath as Junko sat primly on the big flat stone paying rapt attention to his every word. He told her all he knew from what he had seen and heard during the highly fraught day.

"Brave Momo was badly injured, but still able to walk. Her husband received some light wounds, nothing much to trouble a samurai. They have both been taken into town under Sano's care—fear not, for she is an excellent healer, she has put me back together a few times, actually." His right forefinger traced a long, pale jagged line stretching from elbow to wrist that Junko hadn't noticed before.

"They will spend the night there, and I will spend the night here guarding you until I am relieved of my watch. That is all that I know."

"Momo fought off all those river pirates by herself..." Junko said softly, the expression on her face a mixture of fear for her friend and admiration of her unexpected prowess. Her eyes were far away, trying to imagine what that must have been like.

"Yes, it was a most impressive feat. It seems Nishioka-sensei taught her well."

Junko nodded, the crook of her brow signaling that she would think further on that later.

"I'm glad that you were not hurt," Junko told him as she placed her hand on the tiny silver cross that hung from her neck, then ran her hand down from her neck and back across her chest in that odd way *Kirishitan* people do. She stood up and bowed to him.

"Thank you, Hachisuka-san. I will tell no one that you shared your knowledge of the day with me. It will be our secret."

Hachisuka bowed back at her and mumbled his thanks. *Now we share a secret!* he thought to himself, finding that just the idea created a fascinatingly pleasant feeling in him. Then he cocked his ear.

"Is that music?" He scanned through the darkness at the main road beyond the orchards that it emanated from. It grew louder, and they both stared in its direction

"Yes, festival music! Coming from the main square. But why? Why tonight?"

Suddenly a voice cried out from the Tanakas' front door.

"*Onei-chan!* Big Sister! We can hear music coming from town!" Tamiko stood looking out from the *genkan* holding a lantern, seven pairs of eyes flashing in its light from various heights, from Kaki, to Hana, then up to the five remaining Tanaka children, three more sisters and two brothers ranging from age seven to fourteen. "Is there a festival going on?"

Junko looked at Hachisuka, who just shrugged.

"I don't know. It sounds like one, doesn't it?"

The youngest boy, Nobuyoshi, seven, called out in a plaintive tone. "*Onei-chan*, can we go?"

Junko pursed her lips and shook her head.

"No, we cannot. Mother ordered us to stay here and take care of little Hana, and this samurai was sent to watch over us until she and father return."

A disappointed group sigh could be heard across the yard. A small voice rose above it.

"Junko-onei-chan, I want my momma and poppa!" Hana cried out in a plaintive tone.

Tamiko hung the lantern on its peg beside the door and scooped Hana up into her arms.

"Hana-chan, we are all having so much fun since you are here with us! Aren't you having fun, too?"

Hana nodded, but her eyes were growing moist, a warning sign of foul weather to come.

"Yes, but I want to see my momma and poppa! And I want to go to the festival, too!" Her voice was growing louder and shriller. Tamiko looked over to Junko with a helpless expression.

Junko looked at Hachisuka. His eyes were wide and his mouth slightly open, the comical expression of someone who is completely outside their realm of experience and has no idea what to do.

Think fast, Junko. She did, and began walking over to the door, arms outstretched to take Hana from Tamiko, who was after all, still a babysitter in training.

"*Daijoubu yo*, Hana-chan! It's all right," Junko told her in a calm tone full of surety, bringing their faces close and locking eyes. "Your mother and father have asked you to stay here with us tonight because they are very busy getting ready for the great journey with Mr. Blom and Ishida-san! We will all be going together."

Hana quieted, but was sniffing loudly, still fighting back tears. Junko bounced her gently up and down the way one does to calm a small baby; her mother had taught her that the technique still worked well past infanthood.

Hana let out a great sigh, signaling her capitulation to the wishes of her parents. Staying over at the Tanakas' happened fairly regularly, usually on the nights they needed to prepare a lot of *bentos* that a customer had ordered for the following day. Hana didn't think it fair that they said they "didn't want her underfoot." After all, she was just trying to help! But she did very much love the Tanakas. They were really all one, big happy family.

Hana's eyebrows were furrowed in thought, which made Junko laugh because the expression was exactly like that of her mother Momo.

"Can we go to the festival? Please?" Hana asked in a plaintive voice, raising her little hands in a gesture of humble request that she had learned from watching Father Nixi implore the Lord to forgive everybody at church, even though she didn't know what they had all done that was so bad.

The younger brothers and sisters took Hana's pleading as a signal to start up their own whining and cajoling again.

The pity of it all would certainly have broken the resolve of any but the most steadfast older sister in charge, which happened to be Junko. She smiled patiently at Hana, then the rest, and answered in a light, cheerful voice that still held iron in its tone. "Absolutely not. We are NOT going to the festival. We are under orders to remain here all night, which is why Hachisuka-san was sent by our parents and Hana's to help look after us." Junko's siblings wisely took that particular smile and tone as the thinly veiled warning they were. It was clear that she would brook no further opposition.

Junko turned to Hachisuka, who was silently staring at the proceedings, marveling at the deft way someone who was most certainly still a teen herself quelled a potential rebellion by her younger brothers and sisters, who were understandably unhappy at the prospect of missing out on a festival. The music wafting through the orchards that lay between them and the main square was an enticing siren song of fun and frolic, joined now by a plaintive refrain composed of the dispirited sighs and grudging mumbling of disappointed children.

Hachisuka had never lived in a home with siblings. He was an only child and had begun his warrior training at age twelve. It then occurred to him that Junko was staring at him with a funny look on her face, as if she were waiting for him to say something, while he simply stared back blankly like some hapless animal caught in the lamp's sudden glare. He heard Tamiko let out a muffled laugh from the crowd of Tanaka offspring, enjoying his discomfiture as usual, then was alarmed to see Junko narrow her eyes and give a tiny shake of her chin toward her siblings, before widening her lovely eyes at him again. The look on her face was clearly one of impatience, and yes, it was directed at him. The whole affair had been quite mesmerizing, but that broke the spell.

Trying not to think too hard on his sudden strong desire to please Junko, the young samurai stood up straight and called out in a commanding voice. *"Hai! Tanaka-san-tachi!* Yes! Gathered Tanakas! We are all under strict orders to remain here until my relief arrives to tell us otherwise. It's our solemn duty to do as our elders have asked us, for to do anything else would dishonor them, and be a stain on our reputations."

This impromptu and very commanding speech brought whatever further unruliness the mob might have had brewing in them to a swift conclusion, except for Tamiko, who was holding her hand over her mouth, trying not to laugh aloud, which would send the wrong message to the younger children. She had decided Hachisuka wasn't such a bad fellow aside from being thicker than a pine board, and just as moon-eyed stupid over her sister as she was over him. Tamiko was still at an age when the awkward social interactions of older teens were somehow utterly hilarious, although deep down it might have been compensation for being a little jealous. The samurai *was* rather attractive, even if he was a bit of a stiff.

Junko nodded her thanks to him for his support, along with a flash of a grin that only he could see. She was pleased to see it made him turn as red as a pub lantern. *We work well together,* she thought, before turning back to her charges. She gently put down Hana, who was joyfully greeted with a face-licking from Kaki. Her faithful little friend would clean up any remaining tears and already had her laughing merrily. Junko then stood up straight in the same way she had seen the warrior do and gave them all a very commanding look, her hands on her hips.

"*Minna!* Everyone! I am sorry we cannot go to the festival. I don't even know why they are having one." She kept her theory to herself that perhaps one had been needed to preserve public morale, based on the chilling tale Hachisuka had told her. Then her stern expression transformed into a wide smile. "But I have an idea. The hour isn't too late, so let's have our own festival, right here! Go inside and get out the lanterns and festival decorations, and we will eat up all the treats we were saving for the day we are to leave. We can just make more tomorrow. How would that be?"

Everyone blinked for a second, then let out a resounding cheer before scurrying inside, hurrying to do as she had suggested. Any festival, even if it was just in their own yard, would be far superior to no festival at all.

She turned to Hachisuka and smiled proudly.

He gave her a quick, approving bow. "You are a most capable commander. I salute you."

The earnest praise startled Junko into a rather unladylike laugh, which made them both break out into laughter, the gathered tensions of the strange day having finally dissipated. After all, it was festival time!

The Tanaka brothers and sisters, working together without their usual bickering, transformed the yard in minutes. Ribbed rice-paper lanterns of various colors and sizes, all bearing the merry message "Festival," were lit and hung about the front of the house and strung up on a line across the yard out to the gate post. Their happy glow instantly spread good cheer among all gathered.

The musicians down the road struck up a rousing tune. Tamiko started dancing along.

"Come on, everybody, circle up!" The other children fell in line behind her with Junko taking up the rear. Tamiko was musically inclined and an accomplished dancer, so the younger children followed her movements until they were fairly confident on their own. Hana was doing quite well for one so young, although she still kept a close eye on Tamiko, meticulously mimicking her every move.

Hachisuka watched from the gate, smiling at the festivities. Tamiko made a point of leading the procession near him. "Samurai! Join us!"

He hesitated, but Junko said. "I don't think anyone's coming, and we will all help keep an eye out with you as we go around."

Junko's request melted away whatever reluctance Hachisuka may have had. After all, it did seem like everything was quiet in the area now that the river pirates had been so thoroughly routed. With a shrug and an agreeable nod of his head, he joined the procession. Junko watched him dance without looking like she was watching him dance and was impressed. He knew the moves quite well—apparently being a samurai wasn't *all* swordplay and standing guard.

For his part, Hachisuka returned Junko's surreptitious surveillance with his own, keenly admiring her graceful moves and lithesome form. He had never been so captivated by a girl before. The feeling was both unsettling and, he had to admit to himself, utterly delightful.

After several rousing songs had run their course, everyone was beginning to flag, the younger children flopping to the grass first.

Junko came to a stop and said, "Let's take a rest. Who is hungry?"

Everyone cheered, except for Hachisuka, who politely bowed to his dance partners before returning to his post by the gate.

Junko, Tamiko, and their fourteen-year-old sister Etsuko went into the house, emerging a few minutes later with trays full of treats and snacks. Miyako, the fourth Tanaka daughter, age thirteen, and Tsurumatsu, the eldest boy, age eleven, laid out a woven rice mat for the refreshments to rest upon.

Before the younger children could descend upon the delicious food, Junko announced, "Let us say grace." Everyone settled down, standing still with their heads bowed.

Junko prayed in her clear and mellifluous voice. *"Bénedic, Dómine, nos et haec tua dona quae de tua largitate sumus sumpturi. Per Christum Dóminum nostrum. Amen."*

Hachisuka had heard the Latin prayer many times since he had come to live among the *Kirishitan* Japanese in Phnom Penh's Nihonmachi. He knew that the Christian religion, which had come to them from the Europeans, was forbidden in Japan. Such was the power of their faith, these people had left their homeland to take their chances on far shores in order to live by its tenets.

He had been wary of his new *Kirishitan* neighbors at first, but his employer, wise Ishida, ordered his men to never question another's faith: it was simply none of their business. Hachisuka had soon come to realize that the Nihonmachi *Kirishitan* were still Japanese in all respects except the god they prayed to, just everyday people: merchants, craftsmen, and farmers like the Tanakas. This musing was punctuated by the Tanaka children all exclaiming "*Itadakimasu!* Let's eat!" at the prayer's conclusion, then doing so with gusto.

Hana grabbed a soft, sweet *mochi* cake and ran over to Hachisuka.

"*Onii-chan! Tabete!* Older Brother! Eat!"

Hachisuka laughed and took the sweet from her tiny hand. "*Itadakimasu,*" he said before he tossed it up in the air and caught it in his mouth, then made his cheeks puff up and his eyes bug out, which sent Hana into gales of laughter.

Junko joined them, smiling at the encounter, and picked Hana up to hold her at eye level.

"That was very gracious of you to think of our guest, Hana-chan. I will be sure to tell your mother and father about your good manners."

Hachisuka, having had a moment to chew and swallow his treat, smiled (charmingly, Junko thought) at Hana and told her, "Thank you Hana-chan. That was very tasty."

All of this attention made Hana blush a little, and, having momentarily lost her voice, she ducked her head to acknowledge the praise, eyes shining brightly from behind strands of her long, thick hair, which had grown a bit wild and unkempt throughout the festivities.

Junko gazed at the elfin-faced little girl she gently held with great fondness. Would she one day have a daughter as lovely as this? And would she also be the daughter of a samurai? That last thought had crept in unexpectedly and threatened to fluster her, so she gave Hana a happy bounce and said, "Let's go get our guardian some more food, shall we?"

Tamiko was a step ahead of her and was heading his way with a teenaged boy-sized offering of various treats, followed by nine-year old Natsuko, the youngest Tanaka daughter, holding still more. Junko watched them with proud eyes. How they had all grown over the last few years! Junko was three years older than Tamiko, and that gave her a significantly higher rank in the family structure. She knew that someday Tamiko would take her place in charge, and their next younger sister, Etsuko would rise in standing, and so on.

Junko tried not to think that there would come a day when all of her brothers and sisters would no longer need babysitting and felt a twinge of regret to think of their childhood coming to its inevitable end, but also a warm surge of joy at the thought that one day her children and their children would all be looking after each other's children, and little Hana's too.

Tamiko and her little sister placed the food on one end of the wide sitting stone and beckoned Hachisuka to eat, which he did with a gracious bow. Natsuko stared at him wide-eyed until Tamiko began to laugh.

"Oi! Samurai!" She called in her cheerful, but always wit-tinged tone. He looked up at her with a mouth stuffed full of *onigiri* rice ball and said "*Ghaighh!*"—the closest he could get to "*Hai!*" with his mouth full, which made Tamiko snort an unladylike laugh. Composing herself, she pushed her shy little sister forward.

"This is my younger sister, Natsuko. She's nine."

Etsuko froze, but an arched eyebrow from Tamiko helped her find her voice.

"*Natsuko desu*. I'm Natsuko," she told him and bowed graciously.

"*Hachisuka desu.*" It wouldn't be proper for someone of his age and station to give a child his first name. In fact, he had not spoken it to any of his charges, none of whom would even think of asking.

"I want to thank you for guarding us today, Hachisuka-san, it is very kind of you. Here, take this please." She held out her hand, which contained an elegant *origami* crane, neatly folded from thick, red paper. Cranes were symbols of peace and resilience, among other things.

Hachisuka reached out and gently took it from her, holding it up to admire it under the lantern light.

"It is lovely. Thank you, Natsuko-san. Did you make it?"

Natsuko ducked her head in the affirmative, a shy smile coming across her face before she turned and ran back to join the others.

"She's shy." Tamiko stated it matter-of-factly.

"Well, I can understand that. I used to be shy, too."

Tamiko nodded. "Not anymore?"

He smiled in his modest way, his eyes darting over to where Junko sat eating with her siblings, pretending not to be looking at them. "Not on most days."

Ever observant, Tamiko grinned. She had decided she approved of the young samurai, even though he was a complete imbecile around her older sister. *These ridiculous older teens! I swear, I will never be so moony over a boy,* she vowed to herself.

"*Ganbatte, neh!* Keep at it," she told him encouragingly, without mentioning just what it was he should keep at.

They all ate their fill of the impromptu festival repast, then stretched out on the cool grass under the glowing lanterns, bellies full and hearts bursting with joy.

After a while, Tamiko looked over at her big sister Junko, who was covertly watching the samurai with a worried expression on her face.

Tamiko followed her gaze and realized the young warrior looked very tired. After his snack he had returned to his post standing guard near the gate, leaning against the lantern pole, but guarding nonetheless, while pretending not to steal glances at Junko. Tamiko rolled her eyes. *It looks like I have to do everything around here.*

"Samurai!" she called out to him. "Take a rest. You look like you're about to fall over!"

"I am not accustomed to such rigorous dancing, nor do I usually eat this much on an eve. Thank you for your concern, Tamiko-san, but I really must see to the duty I was sent here to perform." He stood up straight and took on a more vigilant pose.

Tamiko just laughed at him. "Do you think that if there was really any kind of danger around here tonight they would have held a festival? If there actually was, I can assure you that our parents would have been home long ago to check on us." Tamiko looked over at Junko, then darted her eyes toward Hachisuka for a second. *You're up.*

This made Hachisuka frown a little and gaze up the road, squinting into the darkness beyond their lantern.

Junko, seeing the opening Tamiko had provided, joined her sister and gave him a concerned look.

"I do not wish to undermine the value of your stalwart service in any way, Hachisuka-san, but I think Tamiko-chan is right. If there were trouble afoot tonight everybody would have come home by now, or at least sent word. I don't think it would do any harm for you to take a rest."

Hachisuka looked a little crestfallen, beginning to wonder if maybe he was taking it all a bit too seriously. Tamiko noticed and knew just what to do.

"Well, *Onei-chan*," she said, turning to Junko, "The reason no one has come to check on us isn't a matter of whether or not we are in danger, it's because they know that we have a courageous samurai here to protect us, so we must be perfectly safe. Safe thanks to you, Hachisuka-san. We are truly in your debt," Tamiko told him in thick, admiring tones, the first time she hadn't simply called him "samurai."

She finished with a grateful smile and head bow that made Junko flash her an irritated frown, worried that he might sense her cynical obsequiousness.

"We can guard the gate for a while and give our samurai a break!" Their little brother Nobuyoshi, the youngest of them all, headed toward the gate wielding a garden rake, with little Hana marching behind him, the fearsome four-year-old once again armed with her ladle. Kaki brought up the rear, barking happily. Nobuyoshi gave Hachisuka a salutatory bow and stepped into the breach between the gate posts, flanked by his cohorts.

"Consider yourself relieved, samurai. Break time!" Tamiko told him cheerfully, giving Junko a not-so-subtle nudge with her elbow before jumping up to join in the game that was just starting, *Onigokko*, a kind of Tag in which the devilish ogre tries to catch the others, making whoever she touches into the next *Oni*. "I'm the *Oni* now!" she called out as she rushed over to them with her index fingers pointed up from her temples to form horns, making the younger children shriek with terror and delight as they scattered around the yard.

Junko gave Tamiko a funny little half smile before rising and walking over to the gate as if to supervise the youngsters who had stationed themselves there. She was coming to realize that perhaps her cheeky younger sister was much wiser than she usually let on.

Junko sat down on one end of the big flat rock and motioned for Hachisuka to join her.

He nodded his thanks to Junko and sat down on the other end.

"I must thank you and your very fine siblings for being such excellent hosts." Hachisuka turned toward her. "Guard duty isn't usually so much fun."

Junko's laugh was a pleasant sound in the warm Cambodian night air. "You are welcome. I hope you aren't too worn out by all of our frolics. My family is a lively bunch, as you can see."

Junko turned her gaze back to the renewed festivities. Tamiko had made nine-year-old Natsuko into the next Oni. Instead of running straight at her older sisters and her eleven-year-old brother Tsurumatsu, the clever young girl stalked slowly past them, staring straight ahead with a wicked ogre grin, as if she were ignoring them, daring them to come closer. They were lively, all right, and clever, too.

"No, never!" Hachisuka reassured Junko. "Actually, it's quite lovely. I didn't get to play much when I was a child. I began my samurai training quite early. It's good to see so much joy and the bonds that you all share."

He ended with a wistful smile that made Junko want to reach out and take his hand to comfort him, but she made her hand stay still on her lap.

"Well, they have certainly taken to you. I have never seen Nobuyoshi work so hard in his young life," she remarked, looking over to the gate where her youngest brother led his small force in a circular march, with Kaki taking up the rear, bright little fellow that he was.

"I heard that!" Nobuyoshi told his sister as he circled closer, pulling a lower eyelid down with his pointer finger and sticking out his tongue at her in a mocking gesture.

This made both of the teens laugh, then Hachisuka proclaimed encouragingly, "You are doing an excellent job, young sir. We are safe in your capable hands!"

This made the young boy beam and hold his head up high, but not before giving his sister one last sour look.

"My hands, too!" Hana shouted as she passed by, brandishing her ladle menacingly before her.

"Indeed! We have nothing to fear with the mighty Hana on duty," Hachisuka told her with a grateful bow of the head that made Hana shiver visibly with delight. Kaki, not wanting to be left out, barked and wagged his curly tail vigorously, earning a back scratch from Hachisuka, who leaned over to give the brave little dog his due.

"You're good with them," Junko told him, looking on with a thoughtful expression. "They really like you."

This made Hachisuka begin to blush and give another of his self-effacing shrugs. He carefully cleared his throat of any emotion that might have colored his speech. "Thank you. That is good to hear. I like them, too."

They smiled at each other, eyes locking again as they increasingly had the tendency to do. After a long moment they felt their faces flushing and looked away, sitting in silence for a little while until Junko broke it by stating, "I will miss this place. Everybody says that Ayutthaya was so much better, but I don't really see much difference. We made ourselves a nice home here."

Hearing that, Hachisuka quickly turned toward her, his brows furrowed.

"You are going?" His voice caught in his throat in a way that that no cough could completely clear away, although he did try. "I mean, you and your family are leaving Phnom Penh with the others?"

"Yes, we are sailing away to Grantville with Mr. Blom. He seems quite nice, and our dear friends the Nishiokas are very fond of him." She turned to Hachisuka and, in a poor attempt at nonchalance, asked, "What about you? Are you going?"

Hachisuka rubbed his temple in thought. "I'm not sure. I hadn't really thought of it until now. I know that our group's leader, Ishida-san, is partnered with the Dutchman and is going. He brought me here from Japan to train me in his service, so I suppose I will follow him there. I know some of us will stay here and continue our work serving as guards for the local gentry while he is gone." The young samurai frowned and put his hands out palm-up in a gesture of uncertainty. "I suppose I will find out. A warrior doesn't question, he simply does his duty."

"Of course." Junko turned to hide her disappointment. Everyone she knew in her close circle was going to Grantville, but there were also people who would stay behind, especially those who had not fled Ayutthaya, to whom the Phnom Penh Nihonmachi was truly home, having come to it directly from Japan. Junko admitted to herself that she had really come to like the good-natured young samurai over the course of this long afternoon and evening. Perhaps even liked him quite a lot...

The rousing game of *Onigokko* raged on under the lanterns' cheerful glow. Tamiko, who Junko proudly looked upon as her babysitting protege and apt pupil, had come dangerously close to the grinning Oni and was pretending to be too terrified to be able to run away, allowing Natsuko to catch her.

"What do you know about this Grantville place?" Hachisuka asked Junko. "It sounds terribly odd, the little I have heard."

"Yes, it does! Well, they say it is a place from the future that somehow came back to our time. No one knows how, even the people who are from there. This is despite the fact that the entire population is made up of great geniuses with all the knowledge of the ages who are able to easily speak every tongue known to humankind. They are a wise and powerful folk, with weapons that make our best look like children's playthings."

"That much is true. I saw Mr. Blom fire a tiny pistol that looked like a toy. It instantly killed all of its targets and never needed to be reloaded, a fearsome thing! Ishida-san is very interested in those," he added, then instantly grimaced as if perhaps that wasn't information he ought to be sharing with the rice farmer's daughter.

Junko noticed his discomfort and continued on as if she hadn't. "There is much talk of other wonders, wagons that need no horse or oxen to pull them, and conveyances that can carry people soaring through the air on wooden wings! There are also lanterns that burn brightly without fire and heat, and they are able to talk to each other across great distances as if they were standing next to each other. It all sounds quite miraculous, but to these Grantville people it is simply their everyday way of life." Junko looked over at Hachisuka, who had a dreamy expression on his face.

"I have often wondered what it would be like to be able to fly. It must be wonderful! I have dreamed I could and am always so disappointed when I awake to find I am unable to remember how." He looked up into the night sky teeming with stars, bright celestial fish scales flashing in the overarching *Amanogawa*, the River of Heaven.

"To be able to fly. That must be amazing," Junko mused along with him, but perhaps a little less enthusiastically than her companion. "Grantville is certainly a land of marvels. I suppose it will be wonderful..." It all sounded so fantastic, and yet that was where she and her family intended to live. How could someone as plain as Tanaka Junko, a rice farmer's simple daughter, make her way in a land of such grand complexity?

Hachisuka broke from his reverie, a look of concern now on his handsome face. "You don't sound very excited. Are you alright?"

Junko sighed, then laughed lightly to break her sudden pensive mood. "Of course. I won't be alone. My friends and family will be there, too, all of us together. Mr. Blom says that for all their strangeness the Grantville people are really friendly and helpful. They will welcome us, he says. They are mostly *Kirishitan*, some Catholics like we are, but their laws are very clear that any religion can be practiced there, no one can be persecuted for their faith as happened to my people back in Japan, the rulers making us worship in secret. But we have been safe here...."

Her voice trailed off into thoughtful silence as she looked over her shoulder beyond their home to the distant shimmering lights of riverboats plying the Mekong River just over a mile away across Nihonmachi's rice paddies. The scene was so familiar. Comfortable. Safe—until today, of course! She turned back to Hachisuka, who was waiting to hear if she would go on.

"Of course, the Siamese and the Khmer allowed us to be *Kirishitan* in their lands, but it was more like they tolerated it, not really accepting us, but never saying we couldn't do as we pleased. Just looking down their noses at us, poor benighted followers of Jesus Christ, the Son of a God from a faraway land none of them had ever even been to. It might be nice to live in a country where we are thought of as average folk of a common faith, not some oddball exceptions to the local norms."

Hachisuka nodded seriously, filing all of that away for future rumination. He performed the Buddhist and Shinto religious rites and rituals of his people when it was time to do so, but had never really thought about it much. He realized that for some people their faith was a matter of life and death, a thing that would make them flee the land of their birth for strange countries across the sea.

Hana appeared before them, her ladle lying on the path forgotten. "*Onei-chan*, I'm tired."

Junko lifted her up to sit on her lap. "Well, you certainly should be! The hour has grown late." They could still hear the festival music coming through the darkness from the main square, but it had softened into the more sedate melodies of the later evening, slowly winding down to signal the celebration's end. Junko looked around to see that everyone had grown weary. The game of tag had ended, leaving everyone sprawled on their backs in the cool grass, gazing up at the stars.

Nobuyoshi still stood his guard duty, but the marching had ceased and he leaned sleepily against the gate post, struggling to keep his eyes open to watch for intruders. Hachisuka stood up and walked over to him, which made the young boy blink and stand at attention.

"Young warrior, you have served us well, keeping us all safe while I took my rest. I am ready to return to duty now, and so I will relieve you. Thank you for your diligent service." Hachisuka favored him with a curt military bow which the proud boy returned deeply before heading up the path to home. Hachisuka smiled after him, then turned back to Junko.

"I suppose your parents will be returning soon. I will stay here on watch until they do, so please sleep soundly."

Junko smiled at him warmly and bowed her thanks on behalf of herself and the other children, who Tamiko was now herding inside.

"Will you be all right? I mean, of course you will, but..." What was she going to say? *Will you be lonely?*

The young samurai returned her smile and nodded. "I will be fine." Kaki, who had abandoned his marching to take a brief nap, awakened and came over to sit at Hachisuka's feet. "After all, I will have Kaki here to protect me."

Junko laughed, rose from her place and bowed as best she could while carrying a now sound-asleep Hana. She then turned and hurried up the path to disappear into the house.

Hachisuka stared after her, trying to ignore all the strange feelings that were roaming through his heart and mind. He reached down to give Kaki a scratch behind the ears before he returned to his post, staring up the road into the darkness with his usual vigilance, but quite unable to stop smiling.

* * *

Long past midnight, the Tanakas left the festival lanterns that were still burning in the now quiet square behind them to walk home in the warm, starlit dark. They knew the way well, and as they neared their home, they were a bit surprised to be welcomed by more gaily colored lanterns festooned about their yard.

"It looks like they didn't miss the festival after all," Mr. Tanaka mused, peering with drowsy eyes at the glow of a white rice-paper lantern hanging on the gate post, the word for festival, *Matsuri*, painted on its side in broad, black brushstrokes.

"Clever Junko." Mrs. Tanaka mused proudly, instantly recognizing the work of her eldest daughter, of whom she was unabashedly proud. "She couldn't bring them to the festival, so she made one for them here!"

Kaki began to bark at them.

"*Oi!* It's us!" Mr. Tanaka called out, causing the little orange dog to come running up the road to them, curly tail wagging so hard it threatened to knock him from his feet.

A young, but commanding voice challenged them from the shadows by their gate. "Who goes there?"

Mr. Tanaka paused, looking perplexed and a bit befuddled by the voice and the question, possibly because he had enjoyed quite a large amount of rice wine at the impromptu festival Ishida had sponsored.

"Oh, that's just the samurai Ishida sent to guard the children," Mrs. Tanaka told her tipsy husband. She dragged him onward by his summer kimono's wide sleeve. "Hail, Hachisuka-san!" she shouted back cheerfully. "We are the Tanakas, come back home."

"*Okaerinasai!* Welcome back!" Hachisuka stepped out into the lamp-light and gave them a very respectful bow, as he would any associate of his very influential leader, Ishida.

The young man, hardly a year older than her Junko, she thought, was a very proper warrior, but Mrs. Tanaka could tell he was exhausted, and knew why, sure that her brood had kept the poor fellow occupied with their antics!

"Everything is in order and all are safely within," he assured them with another bow.

Mrs. Tanaka beamed approvingly at him, and noted that he was quite a good-looking young fellow. "Thank you so much for guarding our home and family. Ishida-san spoke very highly of you and your abilities, giving us the confidence to leave everything in your hands for the evening. I can now see he was correct in his estimation."

Hachisuka bowed yet again. "It was my pleasure and pride to do so."

"I hope the children didn't give you too much trouble?"

"Not at all, they were very gracious to me throughout." He paused for a second before adding "Your eldest daughter Junko-san had them well in hand." Then he added with a hint of a smile, "And she had plenty of help from Tamiko-san, as well."

This made Mrs. Tanaka beam proudly. "It pleases me to hear that, of course. I am blessed to have such diligent and trustworthy daughters. Junko is my rock." She then allowed a knowing grin to appear on her face. "I do hope that Tamiko didn't give you too hard a time. She can be a bit wry at times."

Hachisuka returned the grin. "She took mercy on me, mostly. She definitely has a sharp wit," he allowed with a good-natured chuckle.

"Indeed she does. I know too well because I was exactly like her at that age. My humblest apologies, but you still look to be in one piece. *Shujin,* my husband, let's— " she turned to where Mr. Tanaka had been standing to find he was no longer there. He was now lying flat on his back draped across the big sitting stone, snoring softly.

"Oh dear. I'm afraid he enjoyed the festival wine a bit too much. Nothing new there. May I impose upon you to help me bring him inside?"

"Of course! No trouble at all."

Kaki barked and circled around them as they guided the drowsy Mr. Tanaka between them to the stone-floored *genkan* entryway where Mrs. Tanaka bent down to remove his sandals, leaving him safely propped up by the muscular young warrior.

Junko appeared in the doorway, having been awoken by Kaki's barking. She was dressed in a simple nightgown and stood blinking at the lamplight. Her eyes widened when she saw Hachisuka standing in the *genkan* steadying her obviously intoxicated father.

"*Ara!* Oh my!" was all she could manage to utter.

Mrs. Tanaka patted her daughter gently on the arm and said, "Let's get your *Otou-chan* Poppa to bed." She made the short step up onto the wooden flooring of the main house, and turned around.

"Junko-chan, take his other arm. Hachisuka-san, can you please lift him from behind?"

"*Hai! Seii-no!* Right! Heave-ho!" Tanaka was a fairly large fellow, but they got him into the house and down the hall to the room he and his wife shared. The Tanakas were fairly well-to-do. Many families all slept together in their home's main room, but the Tanaka house had three bedrooms, the girls and the boys divided between the other two.

Once Mr. Tanaka was safely laid down on the firm *futon* mattress resting upon the supple *tatami* rice mat floor, Hachisuka began to head back to the front door.

"Where are you going?" Mrs. Tanaka asked him.

"Back to our barracks. Unless you still require my services."

"You have been of great service to us, Hachisuka-san, and we thank you very kindly. However, you are *not* leaving. The barracks are over two miles away through the dark, and you are obviously very tired. You will sleep here," Mrs. Tanaka informed him in no uncertain terms.

"*Demo*...But...," he politely protested, looking uncomfortable.

"I have already cleared it with Ishida-san. You are relieved of standing guard duty, but are to remain here until morning as a further safety measure—there may still be a reprisal from the river pirate gangs. I rather doubt it, considering how many dead ones I saw piled up today." As soon as she blurted that out, she shot a look at her daughter. *Oops! The tongue has slipped. Silly me, but she's old enough to hear such unsavory facts now.*

The gruesome statement did make Junko shiver a little, her dark eyes growing even wider. The blood she had washed from Hachisuka's clothes a few hours before came back to mind, more unsettling now than it had been at the time.

"Even so, it's best to have a samurai here guarding us and little Hana until dawn, at which time you are released and ordered to return to your barracks. In any case, you will do us the honor of letting us share our humble hospitality with you in gratitude for your efforts today. Am I clear?" The last was said in the kindly, but still stern, voice of a woman who was mother to seven children.

Both of the young people said "*Hai!*" at the same time, then caught each other's eyes for just a second and had to hold in a laugh at the matronly woman's commanding presence, ordering a grown warrior around as if he were just another of her brood.

"Junko, fetch the extra bedding from the hall closet. Hachisuka-san, you should take a bath and refresh yourself. I will lay out one of my husband's robes for you to sleep in."

Hachisuka bowed as deeply as he could in the confines of the narrow hallway. Mrs. Tanaka squeezed past him and headed off to fetch the robes.

Left alone for a few minutes, Junko turned to Hachisuka and asked, "How many river pirates did you kill?"

Hachisuka shrugged, suddenly feeling a bit uncomfortable speaking of such things in a loving family home, as opposed to the barracks he shared with his fellow samurai.

"Well, I just did my part," he told her modestly. "I think I sent around fourteen of the scoundrels to their graves, but I might have lost track. When one is in battle such things aren't important. Just killing the one in front of you, and then the next one after, are all you really have time to think about."

Junko nodded, wide-eyed at the thought of taking another person's life, even though it was a commandment that the Lord seemed to forgive in the case of war.

Hachisuka smiled a little at her, aware of the *Kirishitan* tenets. "It is just my duty. I don't take pleasure in it." The latter was a little white lie that all warriors told themselves until they believed it...mostly.

"*Ofuro wa?* The bath?" he asked then, wishing to change the subject, which snapped Junko out of her rumination.

"All the way down the hall and to the right."

Hachisuka nodded his head in thanks, then made his way to the steamy little room located in the rear of the house.

While their honored guest cleaned up, Junko and her mother laid the extra *futon* out for the young samurai in the main room.

"*Okaa-chan,* Mother, I will go fetch the laundry I did for him."

Mrs. Tanaka's eyes widened and her mouth opened slightly, and she paused as if she wanted to say something but wasn't sure what. Junko understood immediately what was bothering her.

"It's all right, Mother. His clothes came out clean, it is not the first time I have had to wash away a bloodstain, you know."

Mrs. Tanaka smiled wanly and nodded.

"That is true, eldest daughter, but it is the first time you have washed away the blood of slain men. I pray to Lord Jesus that it will be your last." She touched her daughter gently on the cheek, crossed herself, then went down the hall to join her gently snoring husband.

Junko hurried to the laundry room, her thoughts and feelings all in a whirl. She had emptied the red-stained wash water into the thick brush that lined that side of the yard, somehow not wanting to put it down the room's drain as she usually did. She had been quite businesslike about it all at the time, but now, late at night under the candle's fitful glow, with shadows creeping from every corner, the little room seemed unfriendly somehow, and a shiver went through her that was more than just the early morning chill.

I washed away the blood of dead men today. Men that Hachisuka killed.

She had dried the cleaned clothing out as best she could with a hot iron, then hung it up on a line stretched across the open window where the night breeze could reach it. Now she took each item down and neatly folded it on the old wooden table set against the stone wall. She tried to push her thoughts away, but they kept sneaking back, insistent.

Is this a taste of what it's like to be the wife of a samurai? Washing away the blood of the men he's killed in battle? Wondering if one day he won't return home, while his enemy's wife washes his *blood from* her *husband's clothes?*

Junko took a deep breath and let it out slowly to calm herself. It had been a very long day full of intense, unaccustomed emotions. She could no longer deny that she was attracted to the handsome young samurai, and she was pretty sure that he was attracted to her. What was to come of it? Would he be joining them, a companion on the long journey halfway around the world? Or would he just be a memory of the old days back in Phnom Penh, that would fade over the years?

Junko shook her head to clear it, then carried Hachisuka's laundry to the main room, trying to figure out what, if anything, she would say to him beyond "Good Night."

The question was moot, for the exhausted Hachisuka had already returned from his bath and was stretched out on the *futon*, sound asleep. She laid his clean clothes down next to his sword and belt, then gently spread a blanket over him to protect him from the night's chill, careful not to touch him, or disturb his slumber. She smiled to find the red origami crane her little sister had given him placed carefully beside his pillow. Junko rose and headed toward the hall to join her sisters, but paused and turned back for a moment, standing still and silent in the hallway, watching the young samurai sleep.

He was beautiful in his masculine way, his long, dark hair loose now, cascading across his gently rising and falling broad chest. She cocked her head and shook it as if to further deny the feelings that were sprouting there like wildflowers pushing their way up to the sunlight after spring's first rain, then smiled despite herself. Junko quietly went off to bed vowing not to dream of him, but she did anyway.

* * *

Junko rose just after dawn to make their honored guest breakfast, but he was already gone. The futon and blanket, all that remained of his presence, were neatly folded and stacked against the wall of the main room. She went to the front door and gazed out at the purple-lit yard and deeply shadowed road, but there was no sight of him. He had slipped away just before sunrise.

Junko bowed her head and shrugged, with a wistful little smile. She went back inside to get the morning repast ready for her family when they awoke.

Nihonmachi main square
Sunday morning, two days later

Sunday mass at the Catholic church had just ended, and the faithful poured out of the wide doors, pausing briefly to pay their respects to kindly Father Nixi as they passed by.

Ishida stood watching from across the square, standing on the cobblestones near his home's front gate. Yoriaki emerged carrying his daughter, closely followed by Momo, who was recovering well from her recent injuries. The Tanaka family came out just behind them, all dressed in their Sunday-best kimonos. Junko and her mother each gently took one of Momo's hands and said, "Let's do some shopping!" Momo looked at her husband, who laughed and said, "Go on, my wife. I will keep Hana busy so you can carry more items. This is your last chance to buy anything here. We leave tomorrow."

"Thank you, husband!" She laughed and forged ahead, pulling her friends along behind her, followed by the rest of the Tanaka children. The weekend market was set up just down the square from the church and always had plenty of delicious street food, clothing, and interesting gewgaws on hand. Yoriaki saw Ishida and bowed, and the older man raised his hand to beckon him over.

When they arrived at Ishida's side, Yoriaki put Hana down on the ground. She was the spitting image of one of the life-sized little girl dolls the Japanese loved to make. She was dressed in a lovely blue child-sized kimono with a pattern of tancho red-crowned cranes, a symbol of faith and fidelity, with her long, thick, black hair that could so easily become unruly, but today was neatly brushed and tied with a red bow.

Ishida smiled down at her and spoke in a warm tone, "Hello, Hana-chan! You probably don't remember me. You were just a little baby the last time I saw you. My, how you have grown, such a pretty little girl."

Hana looked up at her father, who smiled down and gently nudged her a little to trigger a very polite bow at the compliment.

"Hana, this is Ishida-san, he will be going with us to Grantville."

Hana bowed again and said, "*Yoroshiku onegai shimasu.* A pleasure to meet you, sir."

Ishida grinned broadly, and returned the bow at a much shorter angle as an adult does when addressing a youngster. He then turned to her father and asked, "How is Momo-san? Is she feeling better?"

"Yes, thank you! Sano-san says she is mending nicely, and will be ready for the voyage ahead. We are all very excited."

Ishida nodded in agreement. "Yes, we all are."

* * *

Across the square from them Hachisuka arrived from the barracks, dressed in the clothing that Junko had washed for him and carrying what he had borrowed from Yoriaki wrapped in a bundle. He paused in the shade offered by a feathery-leafed moringa tree that grew beside the road, scanning the sunny square. It only took a moment for him to spot her among the market's merchants who had spread their wares out over the cobblestones on carpets. She was strolling just over a hundred feet away, with her mother and Yoriaki's wife.

"Junko," he said quietly to himself, her name lingering on his lips like the sweetness left by a nectarine's juice. It had only been two days, but he had thought about her constantly, unable to drive her from his mind. She was even more beautiful than he had remembered, dressed in a green kimono patterned in willow fronds, her long, straight hair flowing down her back. To his eyes Junko was a true *Yamato nadeshiko*, a perfect flower of traditional Japanese womanhood. Hachisuka had seen plenty of pretty girls during his travels, but none had captured his attention the way Junko did. She would be a rare and precious blossom in any garden.

Hachisuka then saw Ishida standing with Nishioka and little Hana. Ishida was just the man he wanted to speak with. He stepped out into the sun and began to cross the square in his long, easy stride. He felt Junko's eyes upon him now and turned his head enough to see her standing in the market staring at him, her dark eyes bright and beautiful. He swallowed back the greeting he wanted to call out to her and just gave her a quick nod of acknowledgment before hurrying toward Ishida's home.

Junko found herself frozen in place, the sight of the gallant young warrior having ensnared all of her attention. She had been trying not to think of him the last two days and constantly failing. She noticed that Hachisuka was wearing the clothes she had washed for him, no sign of a stain at all, the thought of which did nothing to ease the knot twisting in her stomach.

Her mother, oblivious to the tension, broke into her reverie. "Junko-chan, isn't that the nice samurai, Hachisuka, who watched over you and your brothers and sisters?"

Junko just nodded silently, trying unsuccessfully to break her gaze from his lithe and powerful form.

"We shall have to go thank him again, such a polite young man," Mrs. Tanaka remarked casually before turning her attention to some colorful and intricately patterned Khmer silks, completely unaware of her eldest daughter's entrancement, her mind focused solely on the bargain hunt ahead.

Momo, however, did notice, and followed her younger friend's gaze with a knowing look. She leaned in close to Junko and quietly said, out of Mrs. Tanaka's earshot, "He is certainly a handsome fellow."

This broke the spell, and Junko turned toward her dear friend, hiding her blushing face from her mother, who was now busy haggling over prices with the obdurate silk merchant in her increasingly fluent Khmer. Junko let out a small, casual laugh.

"Oh! I suppose he is, isn't he?" She replied in a light tone as she shrugged innocently, then pretended to be fascinated by a selection of dried fruit laid out nearby. Momo just nodded knowingly and gazed over at her husband and daughter. This is how it always begins. With denial! She mused to herself, thinking of her own youthful early encounters with Yoriaki, and hid a happy grin behind her still-bandaged hand.

Meanwhile, Hachisuka covered the distance across the square as quickly as he could without breaking into an obvious run, forcing himself not to look Junko's way again...not yet, anyway.

Hana was the first to see him coming and let out a delighted squeal at the sight of her big new friend.

"Onii-chan! Big Brother!" She shouted with glee as she broke into as fast a run toward him as she could manage in her wooden *geta* sandals and with her legs constrained by the narrow cut of her kimono.

Her father took a step after her with an alarmed face, then stopped and smiled once he saw her target.

Hachisuka stopped when Hana reached him and smiled broadly down at the huffing and puffing, red-cheeked little girl.

"Why, it's my dear friend Hana-chan. We meet again," he exclaimed in genuine delight at her enthusiastic welcome.

"*Daite!* Pick me up!" she implored him, jumping up and down so her wooden sandals clacked like a pony's hooves on the cobbles, her little arms thrust upwards to him.

Hachisuka looked over to her smiling father to silently ask for permission. Yoriaki spread his hands out in a gesture of magnanimous sharing and said, *"Douzou!* Help yourself."

Hachisuka picked Hana up and bounced her the way he had seen Junko do, which made her chortle with joy. He continued walking toward the older men, and then attempted a bow when he reached them, now understanding how that simple task was made rather more complicated when holding an energetic child.

"Ishida-san," he said first, directing his attention politely to his employer. He then turned to Yoriaki.

"You must be Nishioka-san. I am Hachisuka."

"A pleasure to meet you, Hachisuka-san. I see you are already acquainted with my daughter."

"Onii-chan is my best new friend," Hana proclaimed proudly, hugging him as hard as she could.

"And you are mine, Hana-chan," Hachisuka told her sincerely, obviously fond of the bonny little girl.

Ishida laughed and clapped his young warrior cheerfully on the arm.

"He's going to be a heartbreaker, our young Hachisuka here. He hasn't figured it out yet, but I've seen all the young ladies eyeing him."

This made Hachisuka blush mightily. Junko, who had subtly made her way closer through the nearby market in an attempt to overhear their conversation, and who had indeed been eyeing him, joined him in that condition, although he wasn't able to see it.

Hachisuka just grinned sheepishly, then remembered the bundle of clothing tucked under his right arm. He carefully moved Hana over to cradle her in his left arm, and let the bundle slide down into his freed hand. He bowed his head in sincere thanks as he held it out to Yoriaki.

"Nishioka-san, these are your warrior garments. Sano-san insisted I change into them when I was sent to guard the Tanakas because my own were..." He paused, noting that Hana was very likely a savvy little listener. "...soiled by the day's activities. She said you wouldn't mind, but please forgive me for the intrusion."

"Think nothing of it! Did they fit you well? We have about the same frame."

"Why yes, they are of the most excellent quality."

"Wonderful! Then please keep them as a small token of my appreciation for guarding my Hana so well and being so kind to her."

Hachisuka shook his head. "Oh, that is very kind of you, but I really shouldn't."

"Yes, you really should, and you will." He gently pushed the bundle of clothing back to Hachisuka and reached out for Hana, who favored the object of her affection with a last adoring hug before returning to her father. Yoriaki smiled at the able young warrior's impeccable manners. Ishida had chosen this one well.

"Hachisuka-san, I am no longer a samurai, just a humble boatman, so I have no more need for clothing of a warrior's cut. You keep them and wear them to glory. It would do me great honor."

Ishida frowned at Yoriaki's latest denial of his former trade and returned to his usual rather stern and businesslike demeanor with an attention-getting cough.

"Well, let me see. Hachisuka, you are just in time. You will be remaining here in Phnom Penh to welcome the new young recruits that will come from Japan to join our ranks and provide them with your camaraderie and leadership. They will need to have a big brother they can look up to, and you have very much shown your quality in that regard, hasn't he, Hana-chan?"

He looked down at Hana and gave her a wink, making her laugh with delight at the attention.

"He is the best *onii-chan* in the world!" she proclaimed proudly.

"Indeed. So, go on inside and report to my majordomo, who will have further instructions for you." He then turned to Yoriaki.

"Nishioka-san, Blom has requested I ask you to consult with your lovely wife once more to make absolutely sure she has requisitioned all of the dry goods she could possibly need to run an eatery for twelve months in this Grantville. It's much better to be prepared, as we don't really know what all may be available there, and what may not, and it will take at least that long for us to ship new orders from Asia to Europe. Blom made it very clear that *shoyu* soy sauce will be a very important commodity that will be in great demand, so I have already loaded fifty barrels of it on my ship, but..." Ishida continued talking without noticing the silent drama unfolding around him.

When Ishida told Hachisuka he was meant to stay on in Phnom Penh he felt his heart fall out of his chest, landing with a painful thump on the dusty cobbles. He looked over at Junko, who was now much closer, to see her pale, stricken look—she had heard.

Their pained eyes locked for a moment until Junko looked away. A moistness was gathering there that gleamed in the sun, and she wiped her face with her kimono sleeve as if to wick away the sweat of the sultry Cambodian afternoon. Hachisuka just stood frozen in place, his mind a whirlwind of wild emotions that he was struggling to bring under some semblance of control.

* * *

Momo had seen the exchange as had her husband, both of them putting the pieces together quickly. Momo moved toward Junko, but first locked eyes with her husband.

"Do something," she mouthed silently at him. There was no mistaking her meaning even at that distance. Yoriaki tried to act like he was listening to Ishida's list of requests, but now his mind was distracted, trying to figure out something he could do to stave off the tragedy that was unfolding before his very eyes. He was just about to take Ishida aside to discuss young Hachisuka's situation, when the young man himself spoke up, interrupting Ishida.

"*Doumo sumimasen. Shitsurei shimasu.* Please excuse me, it is very rude of me, but Ishida-sama, honored master, may I please have a word?"

Ishida stopped talking and turned to his protégé, one eyebrow raised in astonishment at the hitherto unheard-of outburst. Hachisuka was now nearly doubled over in a deep, self-effacing bow.

"*Nandarou?* What is it?" Ishida asked, his voice not angry, but definitely incredulous.

"Sir. I humbly request that I do not remain in Phnom Penh. I wish to accompany you to Grantville. Please."

Yoriaki looked over to see that now Momo was standing with Junko, one arm draped around her young friend, both of them watching the exchange with a mix of wide-eyed hope and dread. Mrs. Tanaka remained ignorant of the whole affair as she continued to whittle down the asking price of fine Khmer silk.

"Eh? I have given you your orders, young man. I need you here." Ishida began to turn away, but Hachisuka went on.

"*Onegai itashimasu.* Please, I humbly beg you! Forgive me, sir, but I am young, and I want to see more of the world. This may be the only chance I ever have!"

Ishida's usually calm and serious face was growing red with irritation. He was just about to dress down the youthful warrior for his impertinence, when it finally occurred to Yoriaki what he could do to help. The former samurai stepped in between them, facing Ishida with a pleading smile.

"Please, Ishida-san, my old friend. Do you not recall our own youths? We are cut from the same cloth as young Hachisuka here, bored with old Japan and its stilted, stifling ways, yearning in our young hearts to find adventure across the sea! Please, indulge this fine young fellow in his heartfelt desire to do as we did, and find his destiny in yet another, even more distant land."

A startled Ishida stared at Yoriaki, who had once held the position of his most prized warrior and military instructor until he had lost him to Momo's charming wiles. After a moment he found his voice again.

"Yes, I do hear you, Nishioka-san, my old friend indeed, but I have already drawn up very careful plans, and Hachisuka's service here is an important part of them, as his role is to help run my operations here."

Yoriaki nodded agreeably, but then said, "It is good that you see the young man's great value. I do as well." Yoriaki paused to glance over at his wife, who was standing entranced by the proceedings. *Forgive me, dear Momo. You aren't going to like this....*

He went on in a clear voice that would be loud enough for any nearby interested listeners to hear.

"Ishida-san, I have spoken at length with Sano-san, who I know keeps your close counsel. She informs me that you want me to return to your employ as an instructor of your samurai. I was resistant, but our mutual friend and partner in this journey, Blom, has informed me that Grantville doesn't have the kind of waterways that will support me delivering my wife's food and that my days of being a humble boatman must come to an end. In fact, he intends to hire local young people who know the area well to handle the delivery section of our operation. I would be what these folk from the future refer to as a 'fifth wheel,' a man with a position, but without a purpose."

He paused to look over at Momo, whose face had grown as cold and impassive as a stone sculpture. *Yes, she doesn't like it, but what else can I do?* Sano was right.

"So, I will return to your employ, but only as a teacher, not as a warrior, and on the condition that you place Hachisuka here in my service, so that I can continue his training and have him assist me in training your future recruits that come to Grantville. I watched him fighting in my yard. He has a fine style already in place that could be honed to perfection over time, and, not to be boastful, I am just the man to do it. Besides, it will be a long and potentially hazardous voyage for myself and my family, and having his sword at my side would be greatly reassuring. Plus, my daughter thinks very highly of him, and I have found her to be an excellent judge of character, even at her young age."

Hana, who had also been listening intently, took this as her cue.

"*Onii-chan, daisuki!* I like my big brother a lot," she proclaimed as she fixed her adoring gaze on her brave young samurai friend, who was currently blinking his own eyes with a flummoxed expression on his face, as if not believing all that he was seeing and hearing.

Ishida stood staring at all three of them, the gears turning in his head with an almost audible click and clack. Then he gave a curt nod and stated in a decisive tone, "Very well, then. Nishioka, welcome back to our ranks, I am very pleased to have you return to us. Hachisuka, you will report to Nishioka as your commander from now on. Pack your things and prepare for the journey. I am sure you will not disappoint him or me. Now, kindly excuse me as I must attend to other business." He then turned, marched to his door, and vanished into the gloom within.

Hachisuka was still blinking, stunned at the sudden turn of fortune. It took a moment for him to find his voice, then he addressed Yoriaki in the utmost of grateful tones.

"*Nishioka-sensei! Osewa ni narismashita!* I am very much in your debt! Thank you for your great kindness to me!"

"It is my pleasure. I will be glad to have you with me on the long path ahead. Now, I believe that you have an appointment to keep?" He pointed with his eyes toward Junko, who was now lingering alone beneath the moringa tree, pretending to study its bark and branches. "Meanwhile I also have some business to take care of. I will see you on the ship."

He didn't wait for Hachisuka's deep bow before hurrying off to join Momo, who was now sitting on the church's front steps, her eyebrows furrowed in deep thought. *Well, we had to discuss this some time. Sano was right, I need something to do in this new place, and helping out in the kitchen never was it.* He put on his best sheepish grin, and sat down beside her.

"Momo..."

"It's alright! I understand! You helped our young friends, and yes, you need something meaningful to do in this Grantville, a man's job. I am proud of your talents, even if I don't always agree with the samurai way, and it will be good for those young men to learn from a man with integrity and kindness in his heart. But promise me this— " She took his hand, while little Hana looked silently on, knowing something important was happening, but not quite grasping what it was.

"Anything you ask, my love," Yoriaki said, gently taking her injured and still bandaged hand in his.

"Promise me that you will only train Ishida's samurai, just teach them. Promise me that you won't follow him into war ever again! I am not a fool, and I can surmise what he has planned, bringing his new Grantville guns back to Ayutthaya to settle old scores. Promise me you will not join him on that mad venture. Promise!"

She gripped his hand so hard he was afraid Sano's sutures would burst open.

"Momo, I promise, with all my heart and soul. I am yours and yours alone. I love you above all else and will never leave your side. I swear it."

Momo released her grip and nodded, reassured by his solemn promise. He put his arm around her and the three of them sat there for a while, enjoying their last afternoon in the Nihonmachi of Phnom Penh.

* * *

Hachisuka walked over to where Junko loitered, pretending she didn't see him coming. The rest of the Tanakas had wandered away down a side street deeper into the market. He was particularly glad that feisty Tamiko was nowhere to be seen. He entered the moringa tree's shade and stood near her. The crowd had vanished in the afternoon heat, and they were alone.

"Tanaka-san." It was all he could think to say.

"Junko. Just Junko. You don't need to be so polite with me now, not after all that! I heard the whole thing. Did you really decide to go just to follow me?"

"Yes. It is also true that I want to fly, and see the rest of this wide world. But I want to do those things with you. That is, if you want to."

Junko nodded, then looked at him, her great dark eyes wet and shining.

"I want to," she told him, then threw herself into his arms. It took him a moment to respond, but then he carefully embraced her, reveling in the warmth of her body pressed against his. Junko looked up at him, her mouth slightly open, then placed her hands on his broad shoulders and pulled him down into a kiss.

It was a long, timeless bliss they savored, knowing in their hearts it would be the first of many such.

Upon their lips' regretful parting, he took her face carefully in his hands, calloused from battle, but capable of great gentleness.

"Koji," he told her, looking deep into her eyes, wanting to lose himself in their endless fluid depths.

"Koji?" She repeated back, wondering at the way his face made her heart feel like bursting whenever she looked at him.

"It's my name. You can call me that now."

Just then they heard Mrs. Tanaka calling from far down the street. "Junko-chan? Where are you?"

They both smiled and released each other. Junko took a step away, then turned back to her newfound love.

"See you on the ship, Koji."

By Tim Sayeau

Rose-Hip & Red Velvet

Tim Sayeau

Grantville

August, 1637

Adina Daoud surveyed her family sitting around the kitchen table. Joe
Russo, her husband, still in his EMT uniform, sat next to their adopted
son, Lorenz Buechner Russo. Seated catty-corner from the guys were the
two Daoud-Russo daughters still at home, Elizabeth Suzanne Russo and
Sophia Maria Buechner Russo. All had their lap-cats: Joe's bluish Bomber,
Elizabeth's tuxedo Tennessee, Sophia's calico Lady Audrey (Hepburn),
atop Lorenz's shoulder, his all-black Brillo, and now, sidling up to her,
Adina's marmalade, Coppertips.

Lorenz, in accordance with the usual hyperactivity of 12-year-olds,
bounced in his seat. Elizabeth Suzanne, befitting her status as the eldest,
at 18, thus the one the others obeyed, calmly regarded her mother. A
recent high school graduate, in September she would enter the nursing
program at Thuringia-Franconia's Tech College. Sophia Maria, 17 last

month, matched her adoptive sister Elizabeth's "adult" demeanor. Joe, years past fearing accusations of immaturity, mischievously grinned at his wife while finger-flicking an envelope on the kitchen table, the reason her family waited.

Propped up on a glass, looking expensive with its thick paper and elegant lettera italiana writing, the envelope deserved presentation on an argent salver, instead of a tourist-trap "Aloha Oahu!" tumbler and a 1990s reproduction "Nifty Fifties" table of gleaming chrome, mint green, and lemon yellow laminate.

"Coffee first!" announced Adina, ignoring her children's disappointment. "Can't be helped," said Joe. "Addicted, y' know. Sad!" he said, sipping his own dark elixir. Distraction provided, he luxuriated in the affronted looks directed at him by his nearest and dearest.

Having finished pouring herself a cup, Adina sat, Coppertips at her feet. Eyes closed, cup to her lips, she first inhaled the beatific, caffeine-loaded vapors, finishing with a gulp of lightly-roasted coffea arabica, the pride of Ethiopia's Sidamo region. Done, cup down, she picked up the envelope, her eyes widening as she felt the wax on its back. There, in red sealing-wax, was a coat of arms: one large chevron and three oddly shaped crosses, all atop a man's head. Reluctant to break the seal just yet, she again flipped over the envelope.

Her name and address appeared in large script, centered, and top left, in smaller letters,

Sir William Davenport
Bramall Hall, Bramall Road
County of Cheshire, England

"Hoo!" she breathed out, surprised. She'd hoped for, but never really expected, replies, considering how stupid England had become—seriously, the next smart Stuart will also be the first one!—but here's a response! Sure hope it's a good one. "Davenport, Davenport," she said, working her memory. She'd posted so many letters—gotta say, the 1600s, sure a good year for ghosts—"Oh right, the Red Rider, Alice the Maid!"

"Mooom!" cried Lorenz, his control slipping. "Open it, open it!" He slid over a letter opener, Elizabeth and Sophia nodding their support. Joe, familiar with his wife, sipped coffee. The cats, all lordly indifference, watched on.

Feigning ignorance, Adina Daoud concentrated on the envelope, uttering, "My, those're some big stamps, of Anne Jefferson. Huh," she said, seemingly impressed by the four vividly colored stamps. "These're good, I'm thinking—Van Dyck?"

"Mo-ther!" called Lorenz, bouncing from anticipation. "Mom," said Elizabeth, quietly reproachful. Sophia, staying quiet, bit a lip. Joe, enjoying the play, smiled.

Aware the best jokes are the shortest, Adina Daoud picked up the letter opener, her movement visibly relaxing Lorenz. Struggling a little, the envelope proving as high-quality as it appeared, she slit it open, extracting several pages, all with the same graceful writing as before.

"Read it, read it!" cried Lorenz, again bouncing in his chair. "Aloud!"

"Manners," chided Adina, shaking white sand from the pages.

Lorenz, eyes alight, bobble-heading excited agreement, said, "Aloud, please!"

Sophia Maria, as bright-eyed as her brother, seconded with, "Yes, Mama, please!" Elizabeth added "What they said!" Joe, confident Adina would, stroked Bomber, the old tom purring approval.

"One moment," said Adina, sipping coffee. "Okay, now!" she announced, reading out loud:

The 1st of July, 1637
Sir William Davenport
Bramall Hall, Stockport
Cheshire, England
To Mistress

"Oooh, I like that!" said Joe, grinning, wagging eyebrows suggestively. "Daaad!" cried Elizabeth, upset, then quoted her grandpa Joe, Mom's dad: "No comments from the peanut gallery!"

Ignoring them, Adina Daoud resumed.

Adina Daoud
306 Brush Run Street

"Mooom!" Elizabeth put her head in her hands. "You gave them our old address."

Adina grimaced briefly. "Oops."

Grantville, West Virginia County

"Mooom!" cried Lorenz. "We know all that!" Quieting down at a sharp finger-flick from Joe, he settled back in his chair as Mooom read on, emphasizing words to remind him, Manners!

United States of Europe, 26582
Mistress Daoud,

"Again, I like that!" repeated Joe. His children, and their cats, all glared: Quiet!

I acknowledge receipt of your letter of the 11th of May of the
present year. I confess, it be a most confusing one, for myself
and my dear wife Dorothy. A cat among pigeons, your letter.
Even so, a welcome one, for the Knowledge presented within.
Preventive Measures proceed, at a satisfactory pace.

"Does he say what?" asked Lorenz, curious. "Does he?"

"Shhh," intoned Sophia, with the full weight of her current five years over her brother. "Let Mama speak," she ordered. Lady Audrey mewed agreement.

Refreshed by another sip of coffee, Mama spoke on.

We First considered the Erection of a Tower, in the Manner
of the Irish Cloigthithe Towers, whose Doorways be Positioned
Several feet above Ground.

"That'd do it," opined Joe. "Ladder in and out, lock guests in, Sir William's safe and sound."

In stead,

"Aw, no!" cried Joe. "A tower, that'd be great!" "Yes!" said Lorenz. "A great big tall tower!" he emphasized, hands and arms gesturing about, downing them fast at his mom's warning glance.

Adina, cup and coffee now safe from her youngest's enthusiasm, read further.

> a Room be now set aside for guests unforeseen, uncertain. 'Tis a gaol cell in all save name. Windows bricked, door banded and riveted, festooned with mortice deadlocks derived from up-time Examples.

"They could still build that tower," grumbled Joe. "Weren't they all building follies, back then? I mean, now?" Ignored, Joe contented himself with scratching Bomber under the chin, at the ideal spot for purr and stretch. Coppertips, catching Adina's mood, flicked his tail back and forth twice before curling it tip to nose. Reassuring him with several pats, his mistress continued.

> Aye, most inhospitable of us, and yet, better that than what your good self foretold. The which lays us on to those who perchance walk these halls a-night.

"Yes! Ghosts!" excitedly cried Elizabeth. "The fun starts now!" she predicted, Tennessee meowing support.

> Regretful, thy letter arrived late, preventing Not the White Lady, nor Maid Alice, from their Doom.

"Awww," said Elizabeth, hugging Tennessee close. "That's a shame!"

Pitiful though that be, 'tis recorded their earliest Intimations
be a hundred years and more past.

"Oh well, then," said Elizabeth, stroking Tennessee as he purred. "That's different!"

Thus, all that can be, is done, be prayers for their souls.

"Good of them," opined Joe. Bomber twitched an eyelid.

The Crying Child be a revenant whose occurrence be twixt and tween—"Oh, nice!" interjected Adina—*Thy time and ours, for the chapel be at my Instigation constructed within the Year of our Lord 1599. 'Tis alaruming, that a child suffer on to the Year 1977. Worse, knowing there likely be no preventing such.*

Adina, glancing at Joe, said, "Yeah, not possible."
"If only," agreed Joe. Their children looked at them: Lorenz uncertain, Elizabeth and Sophia in agreement. Adina read on.

I as a child cried, Dorothy the same, our children cried, you and yours doubtless. All that reside within the Vale of Tears, all must betimes cry. Great pity also, that no solace, no prayers, yet send Maid Alice, the White Lady, the Child, to their Heavenly Rest.

"Or maybe those aren't ghosts, those are recordings," suggested Adina, the Daoud-Russo house paranormal expert.

"Recordings?" asked Lorenz, arms holding Brillo while the feline rubbed his scent upon his lackey's cheeks.

"Not ghosts, they're more like images, sounds, playing over and over, like on VHS," explained Elizabeth, as taught by Mom. "Recordings just are. You can't interact with them."

Holding Tennessee back from exploring the table, she added, "The child, okay, probably is a recording, but Alice, the White Lady, could be too, I guess," she cautioned doubtfully. "Anyway, that's what recordings are, imprints on something, like, like sounds on an LP," she finished.

"Oh" said Lorenz, satisfied. Brillo settled atop his shoulders; their mom continued reading.

> The words of Christ be Certain. "Verily I say unto you, inasmuch as you Have Done It Unto One Of The Least Of These My Brethren, Ye Have Done It Unto Me." In accordance thereof, We Davenports, we ask Beneficence of Thee, Mistress Daoud.

Sharp looks from his wife and children shut Joe up, and down.

> Be there Advances in the Phantasmic as the Mechanic? Such as assure Alice, the White Lady, and the Child, of Heaven? Should there be, then with thankfulness, we request such!

Joe, shrugging, advised, "Go into the light, that's about it." Which got him a pained smile from his wife. "There's a little more to it than that, but all right, not much more," she conceded.

> *To that end, enclosed be an international reply coupon, which the King's Mail assure be funds enough for reply!*

"Oh, that's what this is," said Adina, holding up a half-sheet of embossed, heavy paper. "It's a little odd," she said, pointing to its curlicued script. "Okay, it's a lot odd," she amended, after a closer look at its multitudinous swishes and swirls that nearly concealed its purpose.

Placing the pages down, she waited as the card passed around the kitchen table, the humans tracing words with their fingers, while their cats first sniffed, then ignored it as clearly inedible. Once it was back in her hands, she continued.

> *In thanks for thy letter, Dorothy sends her concoction for honey & rose-hip Small Beer, of which She be Most Justly Proud. I counsell, Be On Guard, many Seek that Aquaeous Treasure!*

Interested, Adina Daoud scanned for—"Ah, here it is!" she called. "*First, gather a bushel hops Tardif de Bourgogne*—but, this can wait," she decided.

> *Thy letter also created confusion past the supernatural, for which we request those Wisdoms, Clarifications, you choose to provender. To whit,*

"To-hoo!" called Lorenz. He had lately read *Asterix and the Big Fight*, and the owl character was his favorite.

> *What be an Eiffel Tower? What Guard be changed, and why?*
> *What be a Blarney Stone? Why kiss that? Central heating?*
> *We, myself and Dorothy, we fret, we fray, we wonder what &*
> *why, why & what!*
> *Most significant, why be Bramall Hall toured?*

"Oh, are they in for a shock," said Joe.

"Yeah, I'll tell them to sit, first," agreed Adina.

> *Mistress Daoud,*

Wife, children, cats, all staring at him, Joe, rolled his eyes and kept his mouth closed.

> *that be most strange, provoking the oddest of senses. The Dav-*
> *enport home open to, beg pardon, Strangers! How? Why?*

"Fair," admitted Adina. She finished her coffee and read on.

> *Yet also, Mistress Daoud, I embrace thee, thy parents, our good*
> *Samaritans! Our thanks, our heartful thanks, for shewing*
> *three hundred-forty years on, Bramall Hall Stands! Strangers*
> *tour our Home? Aye, unsettling, yet! Bramall Hall Stands!*
> *Mistress Daoud, that be a Joy, an immense Joy! Our thanks*

anew, to thee and thine, for this our Joy, our immense heartful
Joy!

"Whoa! Laying it on thick there, isn't he?" suggested Joe, earning pained, pointed looks from his down-timer children.

"Papa," explained Sophia Maria, slowly, carefully. "Sir William is a *niederadel* who has learned his family home, his ancestral Hall, still stands three *centuries* from now. 'Laying it on thick?' Papa, Sir William has not *commenced!*"

"Yes!" said Lorenz emphatically. "Also, his wife sent Mom her old family recipe, that's, that's..." He stumbled, searching for words.

"That is adopting Mama into her family, almost!" blurted out Sophia Maria.

"Yeah, totally!" agreed Lorenz, fine with his sister's interjection. "That's what it's like. What it *is*, almost."

Joe, double-taking between the two, bemusedly asked, "Sooo, should we call her 'm'lady Adina' then?"

"Yes, *peasant!*" laughed Addie, reading on in her best "m'lady" voice.

> *Mistress Daoud, I earlier requested Knowledge there may*
> *be concerning the placating of Dwell-Ins. Mistress Daoud, I,*
> *Dorothy, our Family entire, again request Knowledge.*

"*Noblesse oblige*, m'lady," voiced Joe, accent perfect.
Ignoring him, she read on.

> *We accept that in the Year 1977 Bramall Hall was toured.*
> *Why? Was it Invitation by the Davenports of the time? And*

yet, as we comprehend thy letter, Bramall Hall be but part of
a larger whole, a Medley of haunted manses. Again, Why?
We Davenports, We humbly request what import more ye may
possess of our Family, our Home. Trusting in thy good self,
I remain, Yr. Most Obedient Servant,
Sir William V Davenport

The reading finished, Adina Daoud, husband, and children, quietly considered Sir William's letter, his requests, and his family's. Joe spoke up first. "Well," he said, "well-a-day, that's quite something, that is."

Elizabeth nodded. "Yeah, sure is! What're you gonna do, Mom?"

As eight pairs of eyes looked to her expectantly, Adina Daoud replied, "Answer, I guess, but, hoo boy, this's more than I expected. Calls for thought, this does."

Joe bobbled agreement. "Well, you've still got that booklet on Bramall Hall, right? With all the stuff about them and their ghosts."

"No, that's with my mom," corrected Adina. "But yeah, there's more on the Davenports there—not much more, but some!"

"Oh, I can type that up," volunteered Elizabeth. "Tell them about recordings too, Mom."

"Yes, and,"—Sophia Maria put a hand up for attention—"perhaps send the recipe for Oma Nina's butter raisin tarts," she suggested.

"Makes sense," agreed Lorenz. "Mom got Lady Davenport's recipe. It's fair."

Adina Daoud considered the chances of her mother sharing the Kacere family recipe for butter raisin tarts. The recipe that to this day her mom refused to share, saying "only when I'm gone." "I don't think she'll share it, Sophia. Not even to a real 'Lady.'"

"So, send them a recipe, anyway," suggested Joe. "Plenty in the cook-books, and we could tell them about red velvet cake, too," he offered, with a wicked grin.

Adina gave him a look. "Do you—"

"Yes, let's!" interjected Elizabeth. "Red Velvet Cake, Mom, *Red Vel-vet Ca-ke!*"

"Yes, please!" said Lorenz.

Sophia Maria supported Papa, sister, and brother with "Yes Mama, Red Velvet Cake—that alone equals Dame Dorothy's recipe!" The cats, catching the mood, meowed. Loudly.

"Infamy, infamy, you've all got it In-fa-me!" grumbled Adina Daoud.

Her family gloated at having successfully conspired to have Mom bake them a cake. "And don't you start!" she scolded Brillo, who was still mewing at her. "You know that's bad for cats." Brillo, for reply, blinked surprise that Mom could think he, playful innocent sweet summer child he, would ever suggest feeding cats cake.

Matriarchy affirmed, Adina joined Joe, daughters, and son in discussing what needed typing up, what could be sent as is, what *mustn't* be sent to Sir William and Dame Dorothy.

October 1637
Bramall Hall

Sir William Davenport greeted Captain Crippen, the latter slowly trotting his horse towards Bramall Hall. Behind Crippen, his men, mounted on their horses, awaited his return.

In the weeks since Crippen delivered <u>The Letter</u> to Sir William, the mercenary and his troops had become semi-regular sights at Bramall Hall. Enough so that Sir William and Dame Dorothy warned their staff of the perils attendant upon mercenary life, the likelihood of violent death, "and if naught else, should any, maid or man, haunt Bramall, then bestir yourselves, clean the Hall, maintain the grounds!"

This time, Captain Crippen simply handed over a packet, explaining, "'Tis another from Grantville, Sir William. Aye, all read aforehand, and again, all fine enow! My regards to Dame Dorothy, pardon the haste, the day's a right Murphy, it is," he explained, crossing fingers, and carefully wheeling his horse back toward his troop. "Send us a prayer, Sir William, we're needing it!"

Heartfelt nods from many of his command showed Crippen, albeit likely exaggerating, yet spoke true.

Quickly crossing his fingers—superstitious foolery Murphy, the fabled up-timer imp, might be, but there was no denying some days do wear—Sir William watched them leave. Much as he and Dorothy liked and respected Crippen and admired the good discipline of his men, there was no denying Mur—difficulties rode close to even the best-led soldiers and mercenaries.

Entering through the front hall, he checked the newly installed longcase floor clock, what up-timers called a "grandfather" clock; for Father Time, perhaps? Purchased these two months and more past from a newly established Mancunian manufactory, the Tempus Fugit Horologium, motto *Nam Longissimum Tempus*. An immense confection of solid English oak, bright Sheffield brass, up-time derived innards, it watched over the hall with a—grandfatherly?—eye. As he watched, "Lord Walton", as it had been nicknamed by the younger Davenports, struck the hour, announcing the time with deeply pealing bells accompanied by the equally sonorous hoo-hoots of a carved-wood owl. Ah, at this hour, Dorothy would most likely be...

She was having elevenses within the solar, her name for that particular ground-floor room. Recognizing his footsteps, she called out, "Hello, dear, do join me!", as she placed her book down.

Seating himself, he watched while she poured him a mug of small beer. The current batch was her experiment at copying the taste of Earl Grey tea. Not a success, in Sir William's judgment—too much bergamot—but tolerable. "Solved the murder?" he asked, seeing Dame Agatha Christie's *The Murder of Roger Ackroyd* lying close to hand

"No, this one proves most disconcerting." She glanced at her notes. "Caroline Sheppard is Dame Agatha's jest, Ralph Patton is too obvious a suspect, Mrs. Ackroyd too comedic, though perhaps that be Dame Agatha's ploy."

"The little grey cells unhelpful, hmmm?" suggested her husband, sipping his tea. Like his wife, he enjoyed Dame Agatha's novels. Unlike her, he read solely for enjoyment, not...victory, in a sense.

"At the moment, no," confessed Dorothy. "No telling me, I still have a day," she warned, enforcing her rule of reading mystery novels up to just before the dramatic reveal, then allowing three days in which to solve it herself.

"Very well, but I warn you, this one will prove a shock," cautioned Sir William. His task in Dorothy's endeavor was to read the books beforehand, then tell her at what page to stop.

"Well-a-day, if it does, I shall haunt the library," Dame Dorothy declared. "Myself, Alice, and Lady Petronilla—better there than Paradise, Plaster, the hallways!"

Astonished, then aghast, then amused by her supposed fate, she'd then christened the White Lady, also placing checkers and a chess set in the Plaster Room. "William, consider her plight, nameless, without distraction!

Her tedium alone affrights!" The games to date were untouched, but allow the Lady Petronilla her time.

Alice, the Bramall passageways her nightly domain, was more difficult to, to—entertain? Thus far, Dorothy's only idea was to openly invite Alice to meet Petronilla. Dorothy herself considered that insufficient, but, lacking a better idea, every Sunday night she made the overture.

Strangely, since naming the White Lady and offering amusements, somehow the Plaster Room seemed more open. Nights also, there was felt an ease, a release. Most odd. Well-a-day, "more things in Heaven and Earth," as William Shakespeare wrote. The halls, feeling more open, no-o-o, can't say that, but then, those are much larger; allow Maid Alice her time.

"But enough, what have our friends Ebulus and Daoud brought to-day?" she asked, curious.

"H-How—?" stuttered Sir William.

"A packet in your hand, 'Anne Jefferson' stamps on't, and the day forty horsemen ride near without sounding loud is a day all are inside from the heavy rain," explained Dame Dorothy, serene as only those are who correctly solve five Holmes and Watson stories (*Engineer's Thumb, Silver Blaze, Blue Carbuncle, Thor Bridge, Solitary Cyclist*) in advance of revelation. "I admit, the Daoud be supposition derived from the stamps. The rest, observation, my dear Watson, observation!"

Shaking his head—really, that passing peddler who sold Dorothy a cheapjack copy of *Lord Wimsey, The Noble Detectionary,* must qualify as an apparition, for certainly his presence haunts—Sir William handed her the packet. "God's truth, Dorothy, I fear you shall welcome the Red Rider, solely for the prospect of solving my death!"

Dame Dorothy, peering at the address, shook her head. "No, I would not, Will. Certainly attempt, I assure, but truthfully, fictional mysteries are fair, love. Evidence presented as at a banquet, motives of necessity hidden, yet always comprehensible."

She looked away, over the grounds of the hall, seeing not autumn, but instead a wintry day and in the distance an approaching horseman. She clenched a hand. "There is so *little*, William. No description, no name true or false, naught but a New Year's Eve, a red-lined cloak, a horse. No motive, none, none and nothing! The Rider comes, murders, departs. 'And I looked, and behold a pale horse: and His name that sat on him was Death.'"

Bible study complete, she asked, "Also, William, why would he haunt the hall? Myself, why would I not, considering? But him, why? Was he himself murdered that night?" She thought a moment. "A possibility, a most likely possibility, but then, why conceal his body, why slaughter his horse? More, how could those be concealed? Swear all to secrecy? Impossible!"

Shaking her head, she mildly reproved. "Honestly, William, that you did not yourself become a ghost is grossly inconsiderate." Again, she shook her head. "Myself, the Rider, his horse, but not you? Not the main, the most concerned person?"

She favored him with a wagging finger. "William, how could you not? Such discourtesy! At least long enough to name your assailant, William!" She tapped *Ackroyd*. "As it is, Master Poirot himself would fail!"

Playing along, Sir William admitted, "Yes, Dorothy, as you say, a discourtesy, a most grievous discourtesy!" Holding up a hand as in oath-taking, he stated, "I promise, O My Miss Marple, should it prove necessary, I shall name him from the grave, pursue him as the Furies of Greece themselves!"

Dame Dorothy, sniffing her disbelief, admonished "See that you do, Sir William. See that you do," closing her words with a bright grin to match his.

With that, she moved *Ackroyd* and the notes thereof carefully to one side, the better to study the latest news from Grantville. Smile gone, she finger-flicked the knife-cut opening of the large packet.

Among the beautiful aspects of the Bramall Hall solar was that it could not be quietly entered, its doors always creaking. Another grace was that none outside might listen to those within without being seen. Lastly, right now, only the Hall's owner and wife were present. Sir William thrice quick-snapped his fingers, reminding Dame Dorothy who held power here: not her, and, truly, not him.

Shrugging, Dame Dorothy accepted the correction whilst removing smaller packets, letters really, from within the larger, disdainfully eyeing each knife-cut opening. "My, William, I do believe this be what up-timers reference a 'data dump'! Oh, this surprises!" she cried, holding a photograph.

There, clothed in likely their best, were five figures, all smiling. Two, a woman and a man, were seated on chairs, with a boy sitting cross-legged on the floor in front of them. Standing next to the adults were two sluts—ack, NO, to up-timers the word had changed from "girl" to a vile insult—two young *girls*, best remember that!

Oddly, each held a greymalkin, which was rather—again, remember, these are up-timers! Besides, 'tis a Papist superstition, calling cats evil. (Though how they all have their malkins' eyes straight to the camera be most . . . aaack, leave it!)

Noticing scribbles on the photograph's back, Dame Dorothy and Sir William read those. Ah, so this is Mistress Adina 'Addie' Daoud, her husband Master Joseph 'Joe' Russo, their daughters Elizabeth Suzanne and Sophia Maria, and the youngest child Lorenz.

Also their greymalkins; Coppertips, Bomber, Tennessee, Lady Audrey (Hepburn), Brillo...well. Hardly names befitting familiars, e'en though the original Brillo be highly disposed towards rebellion!

Setting the photograph down, Dame Dorothy and Sir William spread out the various envelopes, each differently labelled—Central Heating, Bramall Hall, and others. One envelope, labelled Recipes, had *Tasty!!!* scrawled on it.

Dame Dorothy pursed her lips. Annoying as it was that some Nosey Parker clerk had advantaged himself—and, most likely, more than one—there was a certain, a certain—hmmm. "I suppose that is a *good* sign?" she hazarded.

Sir William, pursing his own lips, nodded concord, saying, "Ebulus assures all is well, and—and matters *seem* well, Dorothy, and, I own, that word shews a humour I'd not expect, were matters not—"

Dame Dorothy set the envelope down. "If not, we'd know, and no blame to Ebulus for doing as ordered. Which still does not sit right, William," she complained. Softly.

Sir William, his "Yes, well," conveying agreement with closure, opened the Sir William-Dame Dorothy envelope, sliding out the pages it held. Moving his chair closer to hers, he held the pages up. "Shall we, *Monsieur* Poirot?"

"We shall, Hastings," she decreed. "Let us learn what other cats we must bell, dear."

Heads together, the Davenports of Bramall Hall consulted the latest augury from those unlikely oracles, the Daoud-Russos of Grantville.

09 August 1637
Adina Daoud
306 Brush Run Street

Grantville, WV County
USE 26582

To Sir William Davenport, Dame Dorothy Davenport
Bramall Hall, Bramall Hall Road
Stockport, County of Cheshire
England

Hello again, Sir William, hello to you too, Dame Dorothy, and hello again, censors checking this! Be nice and pass everything on, okay?

We, that's my hubby Joe, our daughters Elizabeth Suzanne, Sophia Maria, son Lorenz, plus our cats, we're glad you got my first letter, even more that you wrote back to us and that got through.

Thank you also to you, Sir William, for writing back, for thanking me for my letter, and thank you, Dame Dorothy, for your family recipe. (More on that in a bit.)

Also, because why not, we included a family photo, our names and our cats' names on the back! Okay, introductions done, Back To Business.

Sir William, Dame Dorothy, as you see, this's a lot more than a page or two. That's because Joe, Elizabeth, Sophia, and Lorenz, they all wanted to write you, too. Joe, since he's an EMT, that's Emergency Medical Technician, and Elizabeth since she's go-

ing into nursing, they're including stuff on First Aid, emer-
gency treatment for shock—we figure that's why Alice the Maid
of Bramall Hall died, shock—and some other stuff, too, about
what not to wear, no torture devices like corsets, UGH!

Also, Sir William, you had questions, here are answers I hope
are enough.

Alice & The White Lady = I'm enclosing a bit about laying
ghosts to rest, which I hope helps.

Changing Of The Guard = the guards are those at Bucking-
ham Palace, guarding the Royal Family. The guards change
every day at set hours and people watch that, usually the one
around noon. Buckingham Palace doesn't exist yet.

Blarney Stone = is a big stone set in Blarney Castle in Ireland.
The story is, anybody who kisses it gains the gift of blarney,
"charming talk used to persuade or convince others." I can't say
I did, but, that's the story. Unlike the Eiffel Tower, the Blarney
Stone exists today, but I don't think kissing it's caught on yet.

Central Heating = is about heating homes with a central heat-
ing system, which for places like Bramall Hall means a lot of
tearing apart! We put in some stuff, but honestly, refitting old
homes is complicated. What works for some places isn't so good
in others. Anyway, if anything we included helps, hooray! Just
remember, if you go for central heating like steam pipes, One,
NO LEAD, hurt anybody who suggests that, lead's poison, and,

Two, home renovations always cost way more than expected, ALWAYS! (I'd tell you how I know, but Joe and I, we don't want to remember!)

Eiffel Tower = was built in 1889, it's in Paris, is famous the world over. I included a drawing, so you know what it looks like. Eiffel because its architect was Gustave Eiffel, Tower because it does. It's the symbol of Paris, up-time.

Bramall Hall = Good news, there's more. Bad news, not much more. The booklet on it's really small, mostly filled with pictures, what got built when by whom, my daughter Elizabeth typed it all up: here's the gist, the condensed version.

Sir William, Dame Dorothy, you should sit down for this, because like with the Red Rider, it's probably not what you want to hear. Sorry, here goes. The reason Bramall Hall up-time is open and holds ghost watches, is because up-time, most places like yours had to either open up, sell to somebody with money, or be torn down. Up-time, even the Royal Family showed off their homes; no tours, but plenty of photographs, books, and television shows about them.

For Bramall Hall, your family sold it in 1877. So, 1637 to 1877, 240 more years of Davenports at Bramall Hall, the rest's in what Elizabeth typed up, and now, time for

More On That = Sir William, Dame Dorothy, here's something we—-me, Joe, our children—-We Ask You to Please Se-

riously Consider. Remember up-time, most places like yours either opened up or went under? Well, maybe possibly instead, one day your family could sell Dame Dorothy's rose-hip honey beer? Other kinds too? Please, I really don't mean to be rude here, that really could be a money-maker! Look at Drambuie, that's a high-class whiskey that will first be made for Bonnie Prince Charlie in about eighty years. It's not like it'd be a new thing to do (okay, I guess now it would be) but Please, Consider It!

If it helps, brewing's got to be easier than running a zoo, which's what the 7th Marquess of Bath did up-time. Sir William, Dame Dorothy, I swear, on a stack of Bibles, That Really Happened. I know, we went there too. (The cheetahs are beautiful!)

That's really all I have to say, Sir William, Dame Dorothy. Everything else is in the other envelopes. Sorry for all the improprieties, and hoping everything, anything, we sent helps, I Remain,

Sincerely,

Adina Daoud

Placing the letter on the table, Sir William and Dame Dorothy regarded the latest confusement from their Grantville—friend? correspondent? Pythia?

"Well," said Sir William, nonplussed.

"Indeed" agreed Dame Dorothy, rereading the letter while Sir William perused Bramall Hall. About a third through he exclaimed, "Oh, that's good!" At Dorothy's quizzical look he explained. "Why, Ebulus says everything's fine, dear. Per this, William was, will be, a Royalist. Not much of one, but well enow."

Dame Dorothy, pleased their son William, sixth of that name, chose sensible politics in both old and new timelines, asked what "not much" meant.

Sir William, pleased to explain, said, "His battles are fought at home, Dorothy. Quartering Royalists one year, Roundheads next, as their fortunes wax and wane. Land donated to the king here, a fine paid to Parliament there. Through all, he maintains our home well enow. Indeed"—he smiled, a paterfamilias proud his namesake heir is proven competent—"he steers Bramall to safe shores through the storms. I own, 'tis almost pitiful we live not upon the coast, Drake himself could not better navigate!" Beaming, he handed her the Davenport future.

Dame Dorothy, as pleased as Sir William at learning that their first-born reflected well his raising, cautiously read through the letter, searching for—

She blinked. Rapidly, several times. "*Seven hundred and fifty pounds*? He paid *that much* to Parliament?" Dazedly, she stared at the ewer of Earl Grey beer. "I'll have to brew more," she said, quiet, hushed. "Much, much more!"

Sir William shrugged. "Yes well, that may prove necessary." He shook his head. "Though to brew that much, could we? Mayhap instead, whisky?"

"Mmm," said Dame Dorothy, considering their prospects and reviewing Mistress Daoud's advisements. "William?" she asked.

Recognizing the tone, Sir William, as trained, answered, "Yes, dear?"

"Please call for William and Margaret, also the grandchildren." She waved a hand expansively over the data dump. "Best we share all this now, with them. After all,"—she smiled engagingly—"should we need brew, they will be the most concerned!" Her smile disappeared. "Far though 1877 be, 'tis clear, one day land alone shall not suffice." She bit her lip, forcing despair down. "We disappear, Will. In 1877, we disappear! Lost to history, as our home be lost to us."

"Mmm," considered Sir William. "I...doubt we disappear, as such, Dorothy. But—"

"But?"

Sir William Davenport raised eyes to Heaven, or rather, the thick oak joists of the solar ceiling. "I dislike it, Dorothy. I greatly dislike it. That our family enter trade, but—"

"But better that than we lose Bramall, William! Better that!" cried Dorothy, her face white as the ghost she planned never to be.

"Aye, I agree, which is why I'll find William and Margaret myself, dear." He walked to the solar doors and winced at the opening creaks. Behind him, his wife picked up the envelope marked Recipes.

One quick look, she told herself, as Will closed the door behind him, muffling his calls of "William! Margaret!" "Bramall" will wait till all are here, and truly, it intrigues, what meal could impress spies enow to write—Red Velvet Cake? Waldorf Salad? Peach Melba? Baked Alaska? Intriguing, indeed!

Bramall Hall
New Year's Eve, 1639

Sir William and Dame Dorothy pridefully inspected their three newest children, standing tall upon a side-table.

Research having overcome the reluctance to enter trade—why shouldn't they, when the up-time Charles, Prince of Wales, would himself sell and distribute food grown on his lands?—the past two years had witnessed the Davenports instructing themselves on beer, brewing, and breweries. Their youngest son Edward now headed the Davenport brewing and distilling business, located in Manchester. Mistress Daoud, as an indication of his gratitude to her, held a modest share (three percent) of the enterprise. (Well, well-a-day, 'tis the Davenport family bestirring themselves, 'tis their effort that conducts trade!)

Dame Dorothy, grasping a child by its neck, held the bottle up to her husband. "Hopefully, this be all we see of him, on this or any night!"

Nodding, Sir William took the bottle from her, placing it back upon the side-table, its label showing a man atop a rearing horse. The man's image attracted the eyes: his clothes and his hair—all vivid red—fitting the beer's name, *Red Rider*.

"Aye," agreed Sir William, sharply finger-flicking the image, as though unseating the horseman. "Here, you two, guard him!" he joked, turning two other bottles so their labels faced the rider. One, titled *Lady Petronilla*, presented a ghostly woman playing chess. The other, *Maid Alice*, showed an equally transparent woman, striding through a moon-lit hallway.

"And if not," he growled, jangling keys with one hand and placing the other atop a holstered pistol.

Dame Dorothy opened her mouth, then closed it. No, no arguing, not on this! *Besides*, she told herself, as her husband escorted her out of the dining room. Arm in arm, they turned towards the front entrance, where their son William and the male household staff awaited both them and the Red Rider. *I am no more likely to sleep this night through than he is!*

The State Library Papers
1632 Non-Fiction

Flint's Shards, Inc.

By Iver P. Cooper

X-Rays!

Iver P. Cooper

X-rays may be used for medical imaging and treatment, metallurgical examination, and chemical characterization. How soon will this be possible in the 1632 Universe?

X-Rays

X-rays are a high-energy form of electromagnetic radiation. On the electromagnetic spectrum, they lie in between ultraviolet and gamma rays. Surprisingly, there isn't an exact definition of X-rays, but Encyclopedia Britannica (EB15/X-rays) says that they have wavelengths ranging from about 10-8 to about 10-12 meters (100-0.01 angstroms). There is an inverse linear relationship between wavelength and energy (or frequency) and one angstrom corresponds to 12,398 electron volts (eV) (cp. EB15/Electron Volt; Planck's Constant; Wavelength). Thus, X-ray energies are in the hundred to million electron volt range.

It is also commonplace to speak of X-rays as being "soft" or "hard." Again, there is no established definition, but soft X-rays are at the long wavelength, low energy end, and hard at the opposite end.

Radiography

Film radiography is the process of illuminating a subject with X-rays in such a way as to create a latent image on photographic film. The latent image is then developed and fixed for examination. This takes time, so film radiography necessarily produces delayed, static images of the subject.

As Grantville's physicians surely know, the five basic radiographic densities are air, fat, soft tissue (mainly water), bone, and metal. Air (in the lungs) attenuates X-rays the least and metal the most. The film carries a silver halide emulsion, which blackens as a result of X-ray exposure. So the least attenuated X-rays produce the blackest tone on the film, whereas metal blocks the X-ray and the underlying film remains unchanged (shadow effect).

Digital radiography works by converting light (X-ray) energy to electrical energy. I don't see it as practical in the new timeline 1630s, so I will not discuss it further here.

Fluoroscopy

In fluoroscopy, the attenuated X-rays, rather than striking a photographic emulsion, instead react with a phosphor screen. The phosphor is chosen such that it converts the X-ray energy to visible light. Fluoroscopy permits real-time, dynamic imaging of the patient.

A problem with early fluoroscopy was that the emitted light was of low intensity. Hence, the operator had to first spend half an hour in dark adaptation before beginning work, and the work itself was prone to causing eye-strain. Fluoroscopy also tended to use longer X-ray durations, increasing exposure risks for both the patient and the observer. These problems were alleviated by the development of the X-ray image intensifier (Eisenberg 33). However, that is unlikely to be achievable in the new timeline 1630s.

X-Ray Equipment in Pre-Ring of Fire Grantville

There are no X-ray (or radiologic) technicians (or technologists) who are identified as such in the up-timer grid. We have several general practitioners of medicine and their nurses. These include Jeff Adams (MD, born 1962) and Susannah Shipley (DO, born 1963). We also have one surgeon (James Nichols), but he was visiting Grantville and thus does not have his personal library or equipment. And there are two dentists (Henry Sims, born 1958, and Jaroslav Elias, born 1953), a chiropractor (John Daoud), and three veterinarians (Les Blocker, born 1946; Bentley Alexander, born 1961; Marcia Patton). There are also several physicians who retired prior to the Ring of Fire: Henry Moss McDonnell (1926-1636), John Thompson Sims (1921-1637), and Emery Ellis (1919-1634). These may have libraries but not equipment. A GEDCOM note indicates that the elder Sims sold his practice to Adams.

In August 1633, Beulah MacDonald says that "An X-ray will tell us how bad" a patient's pneumothorax condition is ("An Invisible War," Ewing, Grantville Gazette 2 and II, Chapter 3). An X-ray examination is made by Doctor Schulte at the Leahy Medical Center in December 1634 ("Penitence and Redemption," Carroll and Wild, Grantville Gazette 62), so at least one X-ray machine must exist and still be operational at that time. The Leahy Medical Center did not exist until after the Ring of Fire, so the machine presumably came from one of the practitioners' offices.

On the other hand, in April 1634, Doctor Sims tells George Watson that he doesn't "have the X-rays that would give [him] a certain diagnosis" regarding Watson's "shortness of breath " ("The Boat," Offord, Grantville Gazette 30).

It seems likely that one or both dentists has a dental X-ray machine and that a vet treating large animals has an X-ray machine (probably a portable unit).

Chest radiographs are required for underground coal miners within 30 days of first employment, and then three years after the initial examination. A third examination, two years after the second, is mandatory if the second shows evidence of pneumonoconioses. In addition, these miners must be given the opportunity to volunteer for additional chest radiographs, at no cost to the miner, every four years (42 CFR 37.3, Aug. 1, 1978). Gus Kritikos has suggested that the mine may have a mothballed portable X-ray machine, but it is also possible that the miners were examined at a physician's office.

In April 1635, Jimmy Dick found a fifties-vintage shoe-store X-ray machine in an attic ("Transference," Howard, The Legend of Jimmy Dick, Ring of Fire Press).

As of May 1634, there is no X-ray machine in Jena, despite it being the site of a major university ("Tortured Souls," Richardson, Grantville Gazette 26). But in December 1636, there is one at Magdeburg Hospital (Wild, A Christmas Stollen, Ring of Fire Press). It is not known whether one of the Grantville machines was moved to Magdeburg or this was a machine built after the Ring of Fire.

Radiologic Imaging Training of the Up-Timers

Despite the presence of their X-ray machine(s), it is unclear whether anyone in Grantville has received specific training in operating X-ray equipment. Under West Virginia law (30-23-12), a "licensed practitioner" (physician, chiropractor, podiatrist, osteopath, or dentist) is exempt from the requirement to obtain a radiologic technologist license in order to carry out medical imaging. So, too, is a dental assistant or hygienist "who under the supervision of a licensed dentist operates only radiographic dental equipment for the sole purpose of dental radiography of the oral cavity." However, a nurse in a physician's office cannot operate X-ray equipment unless the nurse is licensed as a radiologic technologist.

If any of the up-timers have received such training, note that it is directed to safe and effective operation of the X-ray equipment. It is not about how to build such equipment.

In California in 1987, in seven thousand facility inspections, four hundred unlicensed X-ray operators were found (Stammer).

Reconstructing X-ray Technology in the New Timeline

Let's start with what may be gleaned from general encyclopedias that would have come through the Ring of Fire (April 2000).

The 1911 Encyclopedia Britannica (EB11) is only of marginal value in this context. I use the 2002 CDROM version of the Encyclopedia Britannica, 15th edition (EB15) as a surrogate for the 1999 print edition. It says, "X-rays are produced in X-ray tubes by the deceleration of energetic electrons (bremsstrahlung) as they hit a metal target...." (EB15/electromagnetic radiation). (While not clearly stated, the deceleration is the result of the attractive force of the nucleus of a target atom on an electron passing nearby.) The greater the deceleration, the greater the loss of energy by the electron and thus the higher the energy of the photon emitted. Since the amount of deceleration varies continuously, the bremsstrahlung radiation is a continuous spectrum (EB15/Bremsstrahlung).

X-rays are also produced when the electrons actually collide with an inner orbital electron of a target atom, ejecting it. This electron is then replaced by one from the outer orbital, releasing energy corresponding to an X-ray photon. This is called characteristic radiation and occurs at discrete wavelengths characteristic of the target material (EB15/X-ray Spectroscopy).

The effect is not actually limited to metal targets; Roentgen first detected X-ray emissions that were the result of electrons striking the glass wall of a low-pressure gas discharge tube (Id.; EB15/Spectroscopy).

EB15/X-ray Tube says that X-rays are produced in a "vacuum tube " by "accelerating electrons to a high velocity with a high-voltage field and causing them to collide with a target, the anode." It indicates that the anode is usually made of tungsten. EB15 also states that the Duane-Hunt Law, a formula relating the maximum frequency of the emitted X-rays to the applied voltage, indicates the then-typical electron kinetic energies were 10-50 keV (kiloelectronvolts). (10-100 keV is suggested by EB15/X-ray Spectroscopy).

The source of the electrons is the tube's cathode. EB15/Electron Tube describes thermionic emission (the Edison effect), in which the heating of a metal filament (usually tungsten) to a high temperature (at least 1,000o C) results in the emission of electrons. The amount of energy required by a given material to free an electron is called the work function.

* * *

Out of four pre-2000 general college physics textbooks in my personal library, only one (Thornton) provided more information about X-rays than EB15. It provided a graph of the X-ray spectra produced when electrons accelerated by 35 kV struck tungsten, molybdenum, or chromium targets (124) and indicated that the work function for tungsten was 4.5 eV (125). It explained why the frequency (hence energy) of characteristic radiation is roughly proportional to the square of the atomic number of the target (165).

A few additional tidbits may be gleaned from Bloomfield, How Things Work: The Physics of Everyday Life (1997), which may be in Grantville literature.

I am not sanguine about the prospects that the schoolbooks of Grantville's electrical engineers will shed much light on X-ray generation, or even vacuum tubes. "The high point in the production of vacuum tubes...came in 1955" (Thackray). Domestic production of receiving tubes began declining about 1968 and was virtually nonexistent by 1980 (Okamura 64). Hence, unless the engineers studied electrical engineering before 1980, their textbooks are likely to give short shrift to vacuum tubes. While Gayle Mason is said to have a library of books on vacuum tubes, these are most likely oriented toward the use of vacuum tubes in radio and not X-ray production at all.

Grantville literature possibly includes "An Inexpensive X-ray Machine," Stong, The Scientific American Book of Projects for The Amateur Scientist, Chapter 3 (1960). I believe it is taken verbatim from the Amateur Scientist column in Scientific American (July 1956, 135-47). It used an Oudin coil for stepping up the voltage to the required levels, and the article describes its construction. An alternative source of high voltage would be a Van de Graaff accelerator. The tube itself was initially "an old radio tube of the 01 type," which had a glass envelope coated with a film of magnesium "getter." The intensity was 0.75 Roentgen units per minute at a distance of three feet, and this intensity was partially attributable to the magnesium. Later, the experimenter had tubes made to his design by a local glass blower. One such tube had a molybdenum cathode and a magnesium target.

* * *

Chuck Riddle, the only practicing lawyer in Grantville as of the Ring of Fire, presumably has copies, either print or digital, of the United States Code and the West Virginia Code, and some safety-related information may be gleaned from their regulation of radiological equipment. If he has a print or digital copy of the Code of Federal Regulations and its West Virginian counterpart, all the better.

* * *

There are X-ray machines in Grantville, and consequently their owners should have user manuals. They probably do not have maintenance manuals; I would expect that the machines were covered by a maintenance contract.

I was unable to find any pre-Ring of Fire user manuals. But the manuals I did find did not provide useful machine design information other than technical specifications (e.g., tube voltage and current, focal spot size, target angle).

Quite a bit of information could no doubt be gleaned by taking an X-ray machine apart, but as long as the machine is functional, this would probably be strongly discouraged by the owners. Not only would they be worried that it couldn't be put back together, there is the risk that the reverse engineering would compromise the radiation shielding.

The best candidate would probably be the shoestore fluoroscope found by Jimmy Dick. The American "machines generally employed a 50 kV X-ray tube operating at 3 to 8 milliamps." If you compare those specs to those in Table 1, it is plain that it is underpowered compared to even a modern dental X-ray tube (ORAU). So, despite Jimmy's statement that "when the hospital found out about it, they went apeshit," I doubt that it would be useful for, say, a chest X-ray. However, it might be worthwhile to cannibalize its phosphor screen.

I would also caution against using its design as a guide insofar as radiation shielding is concerned. "Although the beam of radiation was directed at the feet, a large amount would scatter in all directions. As a result, shoe salesmen received a whole-body dose of radiation, as did anybody standing near the machines" (Wendorf). "The only 'shielding' between your feet and the tube was a one mm thick aluminum filter" (ORAU).

* * *

I turn now to non-Grantville literature: a textbook (Sprawls Jr.) on medical radiation physics, with supplementation from other sources. This is a subject an X-ray technologist would be expected to study, but not a general-practice physician.

X-Ray Tube

An X-ray tube is a device for converting electrical energy into radiant energy of X-ray wavelengths.

The modern tube is roughly cylindrical in shape, with a central bulge. The electron flow is along the axis of the cylinder (usually horizontal), from cathode to anode.

There are two basic tube designs, end-window and side-window. With the end-window design, the target anode is thin so X-rays pass through it. With the side-window design, only the X-rays emitted in a direction more or less perpendicular to the tube axis can escape. I believe that side-window designs are the norm for medical applications.

Over 99% of the electrical energy is converted to heat (Sprawls 127). Heat is initially produced in the cathode filament and then in the focal spot on the anode surface. It is conducted throughout the anode body and radiated to the tube and the tube housing.

Cathode

The cathode is a tungsten filament coil recessed within a cup-shaped region ("focusing cup") that directs the electron beam to the focal spot on the anode. The cup is "highly polished nickel" (Radiopaedia). A small focal spot minimizes blur but also concentrates heat.

I am not expecting mass production of X-ray tubes in the new 1630s, and so the supply of tungsten from the tailings of central European tin mines (the tungsten ore wolframite is associated with the tin ore cassiterite) is probably adequate, even though central Europe has never been considered an important producer of tungsten.

EB15/Tungsten Processing discusses how tungsten is extracted and refined from its ores. It notes that because of its high melting point (3410o C), tungsten is difficult to cast. Typically it is formed into a desired shape by pressing and sintering a tungsten powder. The problem is that this method produces a brittle filament. Coolidge discovered how to make a ductile filament (LAR), but while EB15 alludes to his 1909 achievement, it doesn't explain it. Nor does EB11.

Jack Carroll has suggested (on Baen's Bar) that both the emissivity and the ductility of the tungsten might be improved by thoriation, relying, I believe, on a vacuum tube book attributed to Gayle Mason. The Materials Handbook (897) indicates that "thorium-tungsten alloys have been used for very high voltage electronic filaments." Some older books on X-ray technology do make reference to thoriated tungsten filaments (Ter-Pogossian 131).

The amount of tungsten required for the cathode is small; the filament is about two millimeters in diameter and one to two centimeters long (RadTechonDuty).

Anode

The anode is usually disk-shaped. Tungsten is the preferred material for most purposes because it has not only a high atomic number (74) but also the ability to maintain strength at high temperatures, a high melting point, and a low rate of evaporation at its melting point. Tungsten's characteristic emissions are at 59.3, 60.0 and 67.2 keV (Fink). Molybdenum (atomic number 42) and rhodium (45) have been used for mammography but they are less efficient at producing X-rays than tungsten.

The anode may be fabricated with one material on the surface and another as its core. The preferred core materials may have a relatively low density and high heat capacity (molybdenum or graphite) (Sprawls) or a high heat conductivity (copper) (Glacier Medicated).

Some X-ray machines are designed so that the anode rotates, thus distributing the heat over a wider area. A typical rotation speed (with 60 Hz power) is 3200 rpm.

So how do you rotate an anode while maintaining a vacuum? You certainly don't want an axle piercing the envelope! The anode is spun by magnetic induction. A copper rotor is attached to the stem of the anode. The anode end of the tube is surrounded by the stator, a set of electric coils. These generate a changing magnetic field that turns the rotor. There are also bearings so the rotor turns smoothly.

Because the window through which the X-ray beam emerges is on the side of the X-ray tube, the portion of the anode surface that receives the electron beam is inclined from the vertical. With a rotating anode, the inclination is achieved by beveling (Glacier Medicated).

If a rotating anode design is used, the cathode will have an offset filament and focusing cup, so the electron beam is aimed at a point near the rim of the anode (Glacier Medicated), thus maximizing the affected area.

It is likely that the first X-ray tubes manufactured in the new 1630s will be of the stationary anode type, given its mechanical simplicity. This will limit the safe power output of the tube.

That said, rotating anodes will probably be available a year or two later. Metal ball bearings are canonized as available at least by September 1634 (Huston, Up-Time Pride and Down-Time Prejudice, Chapter 34, Ring of Fire Press). (Lignum vitae wood is a possible alternative to metal.) Induction motors are in full production at American Electric Works in Summer 1636 ("No, John, No!", Carroll and Howard, Grantville Gazette 58).

The amount of tungsten needed for the anode is minimal. A stationary anode may take the form of "a small disc about 1 mm thick and 1 cm in diameter...embedded in a large block of copper" (Dendy 28). A modern rotating anode might have a diameter of 55-100 mm and a thickness of 7 mm (Radiopaedia).

Vacuum

The first X-ray tubes were of the "cold cathode" (Crookes) variety. There was a soft vacuum (10-3 to 10-4 torr) inside the tube (BellJar). The gas molecules were ionized by the applied voltage. The positive ions struck the cathode, releasing electrons, and the electrons in turn struck the glass envelope or, in purpose-built X-ray tubes, a metal target. The gas pressure had to be just right for the desired X-ray intensity and hardness to be achieved, and these were not easily adjustable (Kemerink).

The "hot cathode" (Coolidge) tube, in which electrons were emitted by the heated cathode, was invented in 1910. Gas molecules were not needed (and were indeed detrimental) and so it favored use of a hard vacuum (less than 10-5 torr) (Belljar).

To get a hard vacuum you need a suitable pump. Actually, you may use a fast pump (e.g., an oil-sealed rotary pump, EB15/Vacuum Technology) to get a soft vacuum, and then a fancier one to get to a lower pressure. Light bulbs historically were first evacuated using a Sprengel mercury pump (good to 10-5 torr) (Wikipedia), but in canon a pump scavenged from a refrigerator was used ("Other People's Money," Huff, Grantville Gazette 3). "Breakthroughs" (Carroll, Grantville Gazette 15) canonized the presence of a diffusion pump at General Electronics in March 1634.

Envelope

Borosilicate glass is typical but metal and ceramic envelopes have been used. The purpose of the envelope is to maintain the vacuum inside the tube.

I don't think ordinary soda-lime glass would last long under the thermal shock conditions imposed by X-ray operation. For borosilicate glass formulations in Grantville literature, see "In Vitro Veritas: Glassmaking After The Ring Of Fire" (Cooper, Grantville Gazette 5). For sources of borax or boric acid for making borosilicate glass, see "Borax Bonanzas" (Cooper, Grantville Gazette 28) and "Industrial Alchemy, Part 2: Inorganic Chemical Bestiary" (Cooper, Grantville Gazette 25). Efforts to obtain boric acid from the Maremma in Tuscany are underway in 1634 ("Under the Tuscan Son," Cooper, Grantville Gazette 9).

Window

While the window may just be a thinner section of glass, it is desirable to filter out radiation (visible, ultraviolet, and very soft X-rays) that could fog the film or cause skin damage without any imaging benefit. Aluminum has therefore been used as a window material (Bloomfield 668). Mammography tubes have beryllium windows because relatively low-energy X-rays are used.

The amount of aluminum needed for the window (and added filtration, see below) is small, and aluminum scavenged from discarded up-time sources should be sufficient for making a number of new X-ray tubes.

Housing

X-rays emanate in all directions, so the housing is made of a material that absorbs radiation, except for the window through which the X-ray beam is emitted in the direction of the patient. Lead is the obvious choice of shielding material as it is readily available down-time.

The housing also serves as a radiator to dissipate the heat generated by the X-ray tube. The space between the tube and the housing is filled with oil to act as both electrical insulation and a heat transfer fluid. Cooling may be passive or active (fans or oil pumps).

* * *

According to the vacuum tube timeline's interpretation of the events in "Breakthroughs" (Carroll, Grantville Gazette 15), the "first complete glass-sealed vacuum tube" would have been made at General Electronics around the beginning of November 1634. The emphasis at that time was on maintaining military radio communications, not on radiology, of course. Carroll has opined on Baen's Bar that "GE will be too busy with radio tubes to give much attention to any other kind until some time in 1636. After that, working prototypes of a simple X-ray tube are a possibility."

X-ray Generator

In the trade, the term refers to the electrical system that (1) provides the current that heats the cathode filament, generating a cloud of electrons, and 2) creates a large voltage difference between the cathode and the anode of the tube, thus accelerating the electrons toward the anode target.

* * *

Electrons are produced at the cathode as a result of thermionic emission, i.e., heating a filament as a result of the resistance of the filament to the passage of electricity. The filament circuit typically operates at 10V and 3-6A (Radiopaedia). Consequently, the line voltage is stepped down for use in the filament.

The tube current is dependent on the cathode emission and therefore the filament current.

It is also dependent on the tube voltage, but at the voltages and filament currents generally used in radiology, the filament current is the principal control (Toda 129).

A rheostat (variable resistor) controls the filament current, and this in turn is controlled from the control panel by the "MA selector." The "MA" refers to the tube current, which is in milliamps.

The filament current in turn depends on the filament temperature. One problem is that the temperature needed for good emission is high enough that there is some evaporation of even a tungsten cathode. Hence, the equipment preferably provides two levels of filament heating, a standby level to warm up the filament without causing evaporation, and a higher level to bring it up to the desired operating temperature.

The size of the focal spot is dependent on the size of the filament. It is, after all, an "image" of the filament. To allow a choice of sizes, there may be both a long and a short filament, and a selector switch determines which one is energized (Seibert).

Increasing the tube current increases the intensity (number of photons emitted) but has no effect on the energy distribution of the photons. That is controlled by the atomic number of the target, the tube voltage, and filtration (see below).

* * *

As of the Ring of Fire, American residences were served by three-wire, single phase alternating current, permitting the delivery of either 120 or 240 volts (the latter intended for appliances). Most commercial and industrial buildings received four-wire three phase alternating current, with line-line voltage of 208V and line-neutral of 120V. Some received 480V and 277V, respectively.

There are three problems with the electrical supply from the point of view of X-ray production. First, the power companies do not supply exactly the rated voltage and failing to compensate for this variation would result in non-uniform X-ray images. Hence, X-ray machines usually include a line compensator circuit to measure and correct the line voltage.

Second, the supply voltage is inadequate to impart sufficient kinetic energy to the electrons in the tube in order to produce X-rays by deceleration and collision. To give an electron an energy of 10,000 eV, you need to apply 10,000 volts.

A step-up transformer is needed to raise the voltage (while lowering the current). As will be well-known to Grantville engineers, a transformer consists of two coils of wire, and the step-up ratio is the ratio of the number of loops in the secondary (output) coil to that in the primary (input) coil. In the mid-1990s, a typical step-up was 1000:1 (Sprawls Jr 114). Bloomfield (668) says that a typical medical X-ray voltage difference across the tube is 87,000V.

The secondary coil is preferably grounded at the center point, thus halving the voltage that the insulation around the cables to the X-ray tube must withstand (Forster 16).

Typical tube currents are 50-800 milliamperes (Seibert). With a 1000:1 step-up, that means that the input current is 50-800 amperes. Since normal electrical circuits are only rated to carry 15-20 amperes, either you must install a special circuit that can carry a heavy load or use a small current over a long period of time (10-20 seconds) to charge a capacitor, which then releases a large current over a short period of time (the exposure time).

Since the tube voltage controls the spectral distribution of the X-rays, and hence both their penetrating power and resolution, we would like to be able to vary it. A transformer is made adjustable by giving it a movable contact on the secondary coil, so it can change how many turns the current actually passes through. Because of the high voltage, the main transformer requires extreme insulation (immersion in a tank of oil), and consequently it is not practical to give it an externally controllable movable contact. Instead, a transformer with such a contact ("autotransformer") is placed "upstream" of the transformer providing the final tube voltage. The position of the movable contact on the autotransformer is controlled by the "KV selector" on the control panel.

When the secondary coil is connected to the load (the X-ray tube), there is a drop in secondary voltage, as a result of resistance, that is proportional to the square of the tube current. Hence, the primary voltage must be increased to compensate so as to achieve the desired tube voltage (Forster 16, 30ff).

The third problem is that alternating current means that the direction of electron flow reverses every half-cycle. But in the X-ray tube, we want the electrons to only flow in one direction. So we need to "rectify" the high voltage current. There are two types of rectifiers. A full-wave rectifier reverses the "wrong way" half cycle. A half-wave rectifier just blocks it. Modern rectifiers are transistor-based, but in the 1632 universe we will be using vacuum tubes.

In theory, an X-ray tube is self-rectifying, as the electrons are emitted only at the cathode, and will flow only during the half-cycle in which the transformer polarity accelerates them toward the anode. However, if the target gets hot enough to emit an appreciable number of electrons, these will flow toward the cathode during the opposite half-cycle. This "back emission" can damage the tube components. Hence, even in the 1960s, self-rectification was used only in portable (low-powered) units (Ter-Pogossian 131).

* * *

We do not know the power of the X-ray equipment in Grantville, but I think it likely that it would have been chosen to satisfy OSHA requirements for chest radiography of underground coal miners. Generators acquired prior to 1973 had to have a minimum rating of 200 milliamps at 100 kilovolts peak. Later-acquired generators had to achieve 300 milliamps at 125 kilovolts peak (42 CFR 37.41).

* * *

Single-phase alternating current has a sinusoidal profile, with one peak and one valley per cycle. With three-phase power, on each of the phase wires there is an alternating current, but the peaks are reached at different times. The advantage is that overall current fluctuation (ripple) is reduced. (Note that if there is a fluctuation in voltage, there is also a fluctuation in the spectral distribution of the X-ray output.) The ripple is 100% for single phase without filtration; 16% for six-pulse (full rectification), three-phase; and 3.4% for twelve-pulse, three-phase. (The latter features a phase-shifting transformer to convert three-phase to six-phase before full rectification.)

The most sophisticated power source used on modern X-ray machines is a constant voltage generator. These have circuits that correct the voltage via a closed feedback loop. Nowotny (105) characterized this as a complex technology with high costs of investment and operation.

In our society, the use of alternating current makes sense; alternating current and step-up transformers make possible highly efficient transmission of electricity over long distances, and we have extensive power distribution networks. In at least the first few years of the new timeline, the only place with such a network is Grantville, so there we can choose between single- and triple-phase designs.

If X-ray machines are deployed elsewhere, they may be designed to use "direct current," provided by a nearby power station. Indeed, the machine may have its own dedicated, on-site power plant. A coal-burning steam engine can drive a turbine or pistons, which in turn drive a direct current generator. Direct current does not need to be rectified. The ripple may be reduced by increasing the number of loops in the generator.

* * *

In a single exposure, the heat production in heat units (HU) is essentially the peak voltage (in kilovolts) times the "waveform factor" times the tube current (milliamperes) times the duration (seconds). The waveform factor is 0.71 for single phase; 0.96 for three-wave, six pulse; 0.99 for three-phase, twelve pulse. One heat unit is 0.71 joules.

In the 1990s, a typical anode had a heat capacity of 250,000 HU, but there were heavy-duty versions that could absorb over one million HU. The latter were heavier and thicker and had active cooling mechanisms.

A typical chest radiograph produced 5000 HU (Fink). Heat capacity was principally of concern for therapeutic X-rays.

* * *

The first appearance of a transformer in canon is in the eastern Harz in 1635 ("An Electrifying Experience," Carroll, Grantville Gazette 20). Carroll advises that he "would expect a basic capability for hand-wound transformers by the third quarter of 1631," since "they're part of the instrumentation and controls for the power plant rebuild." However, Dr. Gribbleflotz is unable to procure a transformer in Jena in 1634 ("Feng Shui for the Soul," Offord, Grantville Gazette 17), so we must assume that they are not yet being sold commercially at that point. As for variable transformers, Carroll says that they are "more complicated and in less demand" and therefore might not show up until two or three years after fixed transformers.

Additional Readouts and Controls

The control panel includes a kV meter. This is actually in the primary circuit and thus measures the RMS (root mean square) primary voltage. However, it is calibrated to display the corresponding peak secondary circuit voltage across the tube (Forster 29).

The control panel will also feature means for manually setting the exposure time. The user manual for Grantville's up-time X-ray machine will have recommendations as to the settings for various procedures. A single-phase machine's timer typically operates in increments of 1/120th second (half the voltage cycle).

Grantville's up-time machine may feature some kind of automatic exposure control (AEC). This senses the X-ray beam that has passed through the patient and de-energizes the tube when the total exposure reaches a preset amount. An "entrance-type" AEC is positioned between the patient and the image receptor (film). This is typically an ionization chamber. The ionization of the air inside the chamber is sensed electrically (RadiologyKey).

An "exit-type" AEC is positioned "downstream" of the image receptor and uses a fluorescent screen and a transducer (photomultiplier tube or photodiode) for converting the fluorescent light into electricity.

The exposure is actually initiated by a separate exposure switch. This may be of the "dead man" type, so the exposure may be terminated before the full time has elapsed by releasing the switch.

Air Gaps and Grids

Bone not only absorbs X-rays, it also scatters them. The photons emerge at an angle, and thus the "shadows" aren't crisp.

The lowest tech solution is to introduce an air gap between the subject and the film. The greater the gap, the more of the scattered radiation will miss the film. The air gap is more effective for lower X-ray energies, as those are associated with larger scatter angles. The air gap results in a more magnified image, which may be good or bad.

A grid is more effective at reducing the recordation of the scattered radiation. "It is constructed of alternating strips of an X-ray-absorbing material, such as lead, and a relatively non-absorbing interspace material, such as fiber, carbon, or aluminum." The basic idea is that the primary radiation is aligned with the grid and passes through the interspace material, whereas the scattered radiation strikes the absorbers, but the effect is imperfect.

In an unfocused grid, the strips are parallel to the central ray of the X-ray field. In a focused grid, the strips are "angled so as to align with a specific point in space."

OSHA required a grid for machines used for chest radiographs of underground coal miners.

Collimators

The collimator is in line with the tube window. It provides a set of two orthogonal pairs of adjustable lead shutters that limit the area of the subject that receives the X-ray beam. It may include a second set farther down the beam path. A diagonal mirror is placed in the beam path so it reflects visible light from a bulb inside the collimator onto the subject. The bulb is positioned so the reflected light appears to have the same origin as the X-rays, and the visible light field on the subject indicates where the X-rays will fall. The shutters may then be adjusted accordingly.

Filters

The original X-ray emanation from the anode will include photons that are too low in energy to be diagnostically useful but which, if they reach the patient, could cause damage. The aluminum window of the tube provides "inherent filtration." However, additional thin sheets of aluminum may be placed in the beam path. The required total filtration depends on the beam power (kVp).

If no filtration is present, the Bremsstrahlung spectrum is triangular, with the number of photons produced declining with increasing photon energy. The total number of Bremsstrahlung photons is proportional to the square of the tube voltage.

Note that filtration reduces the intensity of the beam reaching the patient and thus increases exposure time.

Radiographic Media

Like ordinary photographic film (see "Photography in the 1632 Universe: Part 1, Silver Shadows," Cooper, Grantville Gazette 85), the radiographic medium consists of a silver halide emulsion coated on a support substrate.

The substrate first used for radiography was a glass plate. These were heavy, fragile, and expensive, and, since the two sides usually weren't perfectly parallel, the plate could only be coated on one side (Haus).

Sheet film with a cellulose nitrate base was introduced in 1913, and film with emulsion on both sides in 1918. Cellulose nitrate is flammable, and X-ray "safety" film with a cellulose acetate base was first marketed in 1924. The nitrate came off the market in 1933, prompted by the Cleveland Hospital fire of 1929. Also in 1933, it became customary to tint the substrate blue (Haus). This reduced eye strain (Sprawls). A polyester base film was commercialized in 1964 (Haus).

Radiographic film emulsions are typically ten to twenty microns thick, and have a higher silver halide concentration than ordinary film (EB15/Radiation Measurement).

Emulsions may be formulated to give high contrast (a big change in exposed film optical density with exposure) or large latitude (the range of exposure producing useful and visible density values). Large-latitude films are preferred for chest radiography, because of the wide range in densities, and high-contrast films for most other uses. For mammography, you need both high contrast and large latitude, and mammography film has an extended range (on the dark end) and thus must be viewed with a brighter "view box" (Sprawls).

With radiographic film, as with other films, there is a trade-off between speed and resolution. If the photochemical image-forming reaction is fast, the silver halide grains formed are larger, reducing resolution. Radiographic films come in several different speeds.

Since the new emulsions will not have the same sensitivity as up-time film, we will need to calibrate them, possibly by taking exposures of cadavers or animals.

They also come in different sizes. Medical film sizes range from 8x10 to 14x36 inches. Obviously, the film must be large enough to include the clinical area of interest, and will be larger for X-rays of the femur than of the ankle. For OSHA-mandated chest X-rays for miners, the required size is no less than 14x17 inches and no greater than 16x17 inches (42 CFR 37.41).

Film Storage and Processing

Unused film must be shielded, not only against ordinary light, but also against background radiation.

Film processing consists of developing and fixing, and I described the chemistry in "Silver Shadows" (Cooper, Grantville Gazette 85). By the 1990s, it was possible to buy automatic film processors for X-ray machines. I am guessing that the machines in Grantville are not so equipped because the throughput was too low to justify the expense.

Intensifying and Fluoroscope Screens

Typically, photographic film is not as sensitive to X-rays as it is to ultraviolet and visible light (Ritenour). While some improvement in sensitivity was achieved by using thick emulsions on both sides of the film substrate, the sensitivity remained problematic. The solution was "screen-film radiography," in which the film was sandwiched between intensifying screens.

The X-rays not only form an image directly on the film, they also strike the intensifying screen. An intensifying screen presents a phosphor which has a high absorption efficiency for X-ray photons and whose fluorescent emissions match, insofar as possible, the spectral sensitivity of the film (early films were most sensitive to blue and ultraviolet). Not only were these phosphors more efficient at absorbing X-ray photons than were the film, and the film more efficient at absorbing the fluorescence, there was a multiplier effect, in that each absorbed X-ray photon supplied enough energy to produce thousands of visible light photons (Ritenour).

Phosphors containing atoms "of high atomic number, such as calcium tungstate, cesium iodide, or rare earth phosphors," have been used in intensifier screens (EB15/Radiation Measurement). Calcium tungstate intensifying screens were introduced in the 1890s. The transition to rare earth phosphors began in 1974 (Haus). Phosphors are discussed in more detail below.

Both blue- and green-emitting intensifying screens were commercially available as of the Ring of Fire.

The concept underlying a fluoroscope screen is similar but there the goal is to match the spectral sensitivity of the human eye while still achieving a high X-ray absorption frequency. In addition, phosphorescence (luminescence that persists after the exciting radiation is turned off), needs to be limited, as it will result in undesirable afterimages.

Beginning in the 1930s, the phosphor of choice for fluoroscopic use was green-emitting zinc cadmium sulfide (Balter), but I was unable to find a reference to this association in any likely Grantville literature.

Screens vary in "speed." With a given phosphor, a screen can be made faster either by making the phosphor layer thicker or by making the phosphor crystals larger. As with film, higher speed means coarser resolution.

Phosphors

Phosphor chemistry is a rather esoteric niche of the chemical arts, and I would not expect much information on it in Grantville. The geologists may be able to name several fluorescent minerals and look up their chemical composition, and the electrical engineers may know which phosphors were used in contemporary color televisions and computer monitors.

X-ray-induced fluorescence was first observed (1895) with barium platinocyanide (EB11/Röntgen, Wilhelm Konrad), and its fluorescence is green (EB11/fluorescence).

A zinc sulfide screen was used in an early spinthariscope to observe the effects of a radium salt (EB11/Crookes, Sir William; Radioactivity; Radium).

Some useful information is provided by EB15/Luminescence. It classifies phosphors as sulfide-type or oxide-type. In the first category it lists zinc and cadmium sulfide. These must be prepared in "the highest possible chemical purity before the necessary amount of activator can be precisely added." The quantity of the activator ("copper, silver, gallium or other salts") is 0.1-0.001% and about 2% of an alkali metal chloride as a flux and co-activator. The components are melted together at about 1000o C. Silver-activated zinc sulfide fluoresces blue, whereas copper-activated zinc sulfide fluoresces yellow.

The oxide-type phosphors include calcium tungstate (which does not need an activator) and, with manganese as an activator, silicates, borates, and tungstates of the group IIA and IIB elements.

The phosphors used in color television are identified as blue (silver-activated zinc sulfide), green (manganese-activated zinc orthosilicate), and red (europium-activated yttrium vanadate).

EB15 warns that iron, cobalt, and nickel ions act as luminescence "killers" and that even normal activators, in high concentration, will inhibit luminescence.

The remainder of this section relies on non-Grantville literature, unless otherwise stated.

Barium platinocyanide

Water of hydration was contained in the crystal structure and served as an activator. Exposure to radiation tended to cause the loss of this water and therefore of luminescence. Hot, dry conditions would accelerate the process (Properzio).

Calcium tungstate

Edison found that out of over 8000 substances he tested, calcium tungstate provided the brightest image for a fluoroscopy screen (Eisenberg 33). Its fluorescence is approximately six times brighter than that of barium platinocyanide (Wikipedia/Scheelite).

"Calcium tungstate fluoresces in the violet to blue range, which is an excellent match to film. But...only about 3-5%...of the X-ray photon energy is converted to film-sensitive light energy" (Glacier Medicated).

Calcium tungstate is the mineral scheelite, an important ore of tungsten. The Audubon Society Field Guide to North American Rocks and Minerals, known to be at the Grantville middle school, notes (43) that scheelite has a distinctive bluish-white fluorescence when irradiated with ultraviolet light (although it fails to warn that short-wave ultraviolet is needed). This was exploited by American tungsten prospectors during World War II.

Scheelite, like the tungsten ore wolframite, is associated with cassiterite (a tin ore) and small quantities should be available in the tailings of central European tin mines. However, the world-class tungsten ore deposits are distributed along the Pacific Rim, with China having the most abundant deposits.

For phosphor use, calcium tungstate is usually made synthetically. The solid state (fusion) methods involve heating together a calcium source and a tungstate source; e.g., calcium carbonate and tungsten trioxide, or calcium chloride and sodium tungstate. In the chemical precipitation method a water-soluble calcium compound (calcium chloride) and a water-soluble tungstate salt (sodium tungstate) are reacted (Faria). Sodium tungstate may be obtained by reacting wolframite (iron manganese tungstate) with sodium hydroxide or scheelite with sodium carbonate. Tungsten trioxide is made by reacting sodium tungstate with hydrochloric acid (Wikipedia).

Zinc sulfide

This occurs naturally as sphalerite (zincblende). Pure sphalerite, whether natural or synthetic, is not fluorescent, and some of the common impurities (e.g., iron) are luminescence poisons. The first luminescent zinc sulfide ("Sidot blende") was obtained in the late nineteenth century by heating zinc and sulfur in a copper vessel. It was once thought to be pure, but it is now known that its yellow-green phosphorescence was copper-activated (L'Annunziata 1022; Yamamoto 248, 254ff).

Levy wrote in 1935 that "zinc sulphide has never found practical application in radiography owing to the phosphorescence which hitherto has always accompanied the fluorescent phenomenon." He discovered that if 0.5 ppm nickel were added to zinc sulfide or zinc cadmium sulfide, the phosphorescence became inconsequential. However, at a level of 5 ppm nickel, the fluorescence essentially disappears. Additionally, his patent directs that the phosphor should be "as free as possible from heavy metals such as copper, iron, manganese, or vanadium," although silver may be used as an activator. This shows how critical composition is to fluorescence and phosphorescence.

Rare Earth Phosphors

This was an outgrowth of color television technology. The original rare earth phosphor screen used terbium-activated gadolinium or lanthanum oxysulfide. They were at least twice as efficient as calcium tungstate screens (Krohmer). Gadolinium provides green light (necessitating orthochromatic film) and lanthanum, blue light (Radiopaedia).

Barium Lead Sulfate

If there are books on radiation physics in Grantville (doubtful), they may mention the use of barium lead sulfate intensifying screens. These were faster than calcium tungstate because of their ultraviolet fluorescence (AR).

Cassette

The film is held in a cassette whose front cover is transparent to X-rays, and whose back cover is opaque. The two intensifying screens (for mammography, only one screen is used) are inside the cassette and, in a darkroom, the film is interposed between them.

Positioning Means

On a typical up-time stationary medical machine, the X-ray tube housing will be located in a "tube head" mounted on a manipulable arm connected to a vertical stand or suspended from ceiling tracks. The film cassette is inserted into the "bucky" beneath the surface of the radiographic table on which the patient lies, and the table may itself be capable of vertical, horizontal, and tilting motion.

There will be locking mechanisms to ensure that the bucky, the table, and the tube housing do not shift position during the exposure. There may also be restraints or other devices so the patient doesn't move.

Useful Life of Up-Time X-ray Supplies and Equipment

The main consumables of the radiographic process are the film and the processing chemicals (developer and fixer). I discussed processing chemicals in "Silver Shadows" (Cooper, Grantville Gazette 85).

Those practitioners who had X-ray machines as of the Ring of Fire likely also had a supply of radiographic film. If properly stored (shielded from cosmic rays, proper temperature and humidity), it has a long shelf life. It could last a while if used only when absolutely necessary.

Kerryn Offord reports that radiographic film typically comes in boxes of 100 sheets and suggests that a rural physician would probably have one open box and one unused box on hand, ordering a new box when a box was used up. That sounds likely, assuming there weren't big volume discounts.

I do not have figures for the 1990s, but in 1970, the Public Health Service reported that the annual rate of medical diagnostic examinations in the civilian, nonmetropolitan south was 66.0 per 100 persons. The population of Grantville in 1999 was about 3500 so that works out to 2310 such examinations annually. Of course, many of those would have been at the hospital in Fairmont.

After the Ring of Fire, the population of Grantville swells to 15,000 in Spring 1632 ("Birdie's Village," Huff & Goodlett, 1634: The Ram Rebellion) and to 20,000 in March 1635 (Flint & DeMarce, 1635: The Dreeson Incident, Chapter 44). (Editor Bjorn Hasseler advises me that there is a consensus that the population peaked at 30,000.)

Even if the physicians are more circumspect about conducting an X-ray examination and are able to persuade the vets to contribute their supply of X-ray film (as modern vets did with masks during the early stages of the COVID pandemic), the initial supply will be exhausted quickly.

The earliest canonical reference to newly made photographic media is from July 1633, and it is to a "wet" (collodion) plate technique. Dry (gelatin) plates, with substantially improved sensitivity, are available before September 1634. However, glass plates are too thick to fit into a standard X-ray cassette, sowe must either rebuild the cassettes to accommodate them or find a source of photographic film with a polymer base. While there is some conflict in canon, I think the better view is that newly made cellulose acetate film is first in mass production in late 1634 to early 1635.

Fortunately, it is possible to strip the emulsion off both sides of the up-time film and then recoat with newly made emulsion (as used on the glass plates). The emulsion is essentially gelatin, a protein. Pure gelatin is soluble in hot water, but the film emulsion likely contains hardening agents.

Sodium hypochlorite bleach has been used to remove emulsions from radiographic film (Kirkpatrick). Dr. Phil makes bleach ("Ethereal Essence of Common Salt") in 1633, by electrolysis of a sodium chloride solution ("Dr. Phil's Amazing Lightning Crystal," Offord, Grantville Gazette 6).

Chlorine is produced at the anode and hydrogen and hydroxide at the cathode. The chlorine then reacts with the hydroxide to produce some hypochlorite. I haven't found any canonical reference to its production earlier, but the starting materials are available from 1631 on.

The likely procedure is to use clothespins to suspend film sheets by their corners, in a hot water bath (to soften the gelatin), then move them to a bleach solution (to remove the gelatin and silver), and finally to a cold water rinse (to remove the bleach). With a suitable suspension rack you could process several sheets simultaneously.

It is possible that merely dipping the sheets in bleach isn't sufficient. The bleach may have to be rubbed on with a sponge or cloth. If so, the production of emulsion-stripped film will be slower.

The residents of Grantville are still going to have it tough from the time they run out of up-time film until they first manufacture gelatin silver emulsions. Furthermore, those new timeline emulsions are likely to be sensitive only to blue light and shorter wavelengths (thus, not usable with green-fluorescing intensifying screens) and be of overall sensitivity substantially inferior to modern film.

* * *

The remaining useful life of the X-ray machine(s), as of the Ring of Fire, is unknown. We don't know the age of the machines, and we don't know how much they have been used.

In 2014, the European Society of Radiology recommended that general radiography equipment be replaced after 10-14 years. However, that recommendation assumed a much higher level of use than is likely to be the case for the X-ray machines in Grantville. Their middle case was a machine used to conduct 10,000 to 20,000 exams per year, in which case it should be replaced after twelve years, and their low end case was for one conducting less than 10,000 exams to be replaced after fourteen years (ESR).

But as explained above, I think that pre-Ring of Fire Grantville was averaging about 2,300 exams per year, and it is likely that many of those were conducted at the hospital in Fairmont. Also, the practice in Europe in 2014 is not necessarily that in America in the 1980s and 1990s. So it would not surprise me if the X-ray machine in Grantville was more than seven years old. (Although it is possible that it is a new machine that Dr. Adams bought on a financing plan when he took over Sims' practice.)

Radiologist Scott Mattox posted on Quora that his institution had some analog X-ray machines that lasted forty to fifty years. Engineer Doug Binghmam agreed that they can last up to thirty to forty years. Electronic technician John Peterson added that "the analog X-ray machine should last many years, as long as the X-ray tube is replaced when needed," and that depends on how many hours it is used.

In guessing how soon the machine will need to be replaced, we must also consider how circumstances have changed. It will not be replaced in the new timeline because it is "no longer state of the art," because any new machine is going to be "geared down." On the other hand, the availability of spare parts for repairs is in question. It is something of a race: can the skilled workers in Grantville fabricate the spare parts before the machine goes idle for lack of them?

Perhaps the most critical and difficult-to-replace part is the X-ray tube. X-ray tubes have a limited life. The tungsten filament slowly evaporates. The tungsten vapor may deposit onto the insulating surfaces, causing arcing. The gas-metal joints fatigue and allow ingress of air. The target may crack as a result of thermal stress. The lubrication of the bearings on rotating anodes may wear off, leading to binding or jamming. Improper operation may accelerate failure (Spellman).

The most accurate measure of tube life expectancy is milliampere-seconds (mAs) as it reflects both the duration of the exposure and the current

---

to which the tube was subjected. I could not find any milliampere-second ratings for general radiology tubes. For CT tubes, I see life spans of 50-150 million mAs (BlockImaging, Erdi). But a CT scan of a chest delivers about seventy times the dose of an ordinary chest X-ray. So I am guessing that a general radiology tube would have a lifespan of perhaps 700,000-2,100,000 mAs. If a chest X-ray is 10 mAs, that would still be one to two hundred thousand scans.

If I approach it based on the heat unit rating, it is reported that a 4 MHU tube will last 70-100 million mAs (Harmonay). A 250,000 HU general radiology tube then should last 700,000 to 1,000,000 mAs. That would still be seventy to one hundred thousand scans.

McGuire (652) says that "an X-ray tube should last for about 50,000 exposures and is expected to have a lifetime of about 10 years." The implicit assumption is 5,000 exposures a year, which is probably high for the X-ray machine in up-time Grantville. And McGuire doesn't clarify what an "exposure" is in milliampere-seconds.

"Technique Factors" selection

The technical factors (operational settings) affect tube life, image quality, and patient radiation exposure.

Manufacturers of X-ray tubes provide tube rating charts, although it is not guaranteed that they will be in the operator's manual. These show, for a specific focal spot size setting and rotating anode speed, the permissible combinations of tube voltage, tube current, and exposure time, and these are unique to each tube model. It is possible that the control panel of Grantville's X-ray machine will give an error message if you try to set a "technique" that would damage the tube, but that depends on the age of the machine.

Manufacturers also provide anode heat capacity (in heat units or kilo-joules) and heating and cooling curves. These are relevant to the time interval between exposures.

To obtain an adequate image, a sufficient number of X-ray photons must strike the film.

The greater the attenuation by the patient's body (a function of thickness and radiologic density), the more photons must be pumped out by the tube. The total photon output is proportional to the product of the tube current (milliamperes) and the exposure time. Double one and halve the other, and the dose to the patient and the film exposure remain constant. You may use a high tube current to permit a short exposure time (reducing blur from patient movement), provided you do not exceed the heat handling capability of the tube.

There are two fundamental ethical principles: (1) the X-ray examination should "use techniques that are adjusted to administer the lowest radiation dose...adequate for diagnosis or intervention," and (2) the "procedure should be judged to do more good ... than harm...to the individual patient" (FDA).

For Grantville's X-ray machines, the operator's manual should include a table specifying the recommended technical factors settings (peak kilovoltage, milliampere-seconds) for a given examination (adult versus pediatric; body part view and thickness) and setup (intensifying screen speed and subject-image distance). For example, Ecotron suggests that for anterior-posterior view of a 22-24 cm adult chest, with a Lanex 400 speed screen and 40-inch distance, their EPX mobile system be set to 80 KVp and 1.6 mAs. The resulting subject dose is 19.24 micro-Grays per square meter.

The catch, of course, is that this table assumes modern radiographic film. New timeline emulsions are likely to be less sensitive and thus require increasing the intensity (milliampere-seconds).

I would suggest that before the modern film emulsion is used up, the technician should calibrate the new emulsions. One could, for example, image the same cadaver (or an animal, or an elderly volunteer) with both the up-time and down-time film and observe the image quality. Then bump up the intensity with the down-time film until the desired result is achieved.

Since the spectral distribution varies with the tube voltage, and the response of film is not constant over a range of photon energies, this ideally would be done with each of the common voltage settings.

Even then, we have failed to take into account differences between up-time and new timeline development chemistry and batch variation on the new emulsions.

Radiation Doses and Risks

Radiation exposure is measured in roentgens (a measure of air ionization), absorbed dose in grays (joules/kilogram body mass) or rads, and dose equivalents in sieverts (the biological effect of one gray of absorbed dose of hard X-rays) or rems.

The annual exposure of modern Americans to radiation from natural sources is about 3 millisieverts, and the largest background source is radon. By way of comparison, a modern chest X-ray is about 0.1 millisieverts, a mammogram 0.4, and a CT scan of the abdomen and pelvis 10 (ACS).

A 2004 UK study found that only 27.5% of 240 doctors at a hospital answered correctly at least 45% of the questions on a multiple choice test of knowledge of terrestrial and medical radiation exposure (Jacob). In Norway, in 2010, "most GPs showed poor knowledge of radiation doses and associated risks" (Kada). There are similar results in other countries, including the United States.

The switch to new, less-sensitive emulsions will mean that tube current or exposure times will need to be increased relative to what was done up-time. This will mean that patients will get a larger radiation dose.

Radiation Protection

Since there were X-ray machines in Grantville as of the Ring of Fire, it is safe to assume that these machines were installed and operated in accordance with federal and West Virginia radiation safety regulations, and that the relevant practitioners have copies of those regulations in their files.

In West Virginia, there are different regulations for fluoroscopic, diagnostic, mobile diagnostic, dental, therapeutic, and veterinary installations. I assume that the X-ray machine identified in canon was a diagnostic installation. The requirements are in 64 CSR 23-7.3.3, amended in 1983.

Equipment

The protective tube housing is of the diagnostic type (limits leakage radiation at maximum power and one meter distance from the target to 100 milliroentgens/hour). Collimators are provided so that the projected beam can be restricted to an area only an inch or two greater than the film dimension. The controls must provide for turning off the beam at a preset time interval or exposure. The exposure switch must be arranged so it cannot be conveniently operated outside a shielded area. The control panel must include control settings and meters indicating the physical factors of the exposure. The total filtration is at least 0.5 mm aluminum-equivalent for peak operating voltage below 50 kVp; 1.5 for 50-70 kVp, and 2.5 for above 70 kVp.

Structural shielding

The operator's station at the control is behind a protective barrier. A window of lead-equivalent glass or a mirror system is placed so the operator can see the patient during the exposure without having to leave the shielded area. All wall, floor, and ceiling areas of the radiographic room that can be struck by the useful beam are provided with primary protective barriers (those in walls having a minimum height of seven feet), and the remainder are provided with secondary protective barriers. (These barriers are functionally defined; they must limit radiation doses to individuals in unrestricted areas to not more than 2 millirems in any one hour and 100 in any seven consecutive days. And to not more than 2.25 rems per calendar quarter for individuals in restricted areas.)

Operating procedures

The useful beam is restricted to the area of clinical interest. The patient is provided with gonadal shielding (0.25 mm lead equivalent) unless that would interfere with the procedure. Only individuals required for the procedure are in the radiographic room during the exposure, and these are provided with protective devices. If the patient must be held in position, mechanical supporting or restraining devices should be used if possible.

* * *

Grantville's power plant had analytical X-ray equipment and this would have been subject to section 10 of the radiological health rules.

Radiation Monitoring (Dosimetry)

The West Virginia regulations for industrial radiography—which it presumes to be using radioactive sources—require that the radiographer or radiographer's assistant, during radiographic operations, "wear a film badge and either a pocket dosimeter or pocket chamber." The latter are required to be able to measure exposures up to at least 200 milliroentgens. The pocket devices are read daily and, if discharged beyond their range, the film badge is immediately processed (9.4.3). They also require physical radiation surveys after each radiographic exposure, to make sure the radioactive source has been returned to its shielded storage.

I expect that there will be some uncertainty as to the susceptibility to leakage of X-ray machines manufactured in the new timeline, as well as the adequacy of the protective barriers. This may lead local governments to apply similar personal and site monitoring requirements to diagnostic X-ray installations.

A film badge dosimeter contains X-ray sensitive film. When developed, its optical density is compared to that of developed identical reference film exposed to known radiation doses. EB15/Radiation Monitoring notes that the film may be wrapped in thin metal foil to adjust for certain nonlinearities in the silver halide response to X-rays. Also, since the film has limited exposure latitude, the badge can be fitted with a filter consisting of X-ray absorbent strips of different thickness. Hence, the underlying film will have different exposure ranges depending on the filtration (EB15/Radiation Monitoring).

There are two problems with the film badge dosimeter. First, we need some other, more accurate means of measuring radiation dose in order to calibrate the reference films. Second, the film badge dosimeter does not provide a real-time report of exposure.

* * *

The heart of a direct-read pocket dosimeter is an ionization chamber. In an ionization chamber, electrodes are arranged on opposite "sides" of a gas-filled volume. Applying a voltage difference to the electrodes creates an electric field. If X-ray radiation strikes the tube, the gas molecules are ionized, with the cations drifting to one electrode and the freed electrons to the other. The resulting current may be measured. (The voltage must be high enough so that the current is dependent only on incident radiation, not the applied voltage.) (EB15/Radiation Measurement).

If the electric field is strong enough, the freed electrons have enough energy to ionize gas molecules themselves (secondary ionization). This creates a cascade ("Townsend avalanche") that multiplies the signal substantially. The trick is to make sure that the signal remains proportional to the incident radiation. Generally, the "proportional counter" is constructed as a thin wire anode inside a cylindrical cathode. Also, we do not want the gas molecules to incorporate any of the free electrons, and so the fill gas is preferably a noble gas such as argon (Id.).

A metal-coated quartz fiber is attached to the wire anode. When the voltage is first applied, both the wire anode and the metal coating are positively charged, and the quartz fiber is deflected. As electrons arrive at the anode as a result of the X-ray interaction with the fill gas, the net positive charge is reduced, and the fiber moves toward a neutral position (ISU).

The pocket dosimeter has the advantages of being reusable and providing an instantaneous readout (the position of the fiber is viewed through a lens, against a light source). However, it does not provide a permanent record of the exposure.

* * *

The Geiger counter is essentially an ionization chamber (Geiger-Müller tube) with proportional counting and a visual or auditory readout.

Medical Radiograph Interpretation

"Medical students are exposed to the interpretation of radiographic studies only sporadically during their education, and very few U.S. medical schools have required radiology clerkships" (Holt). In medical school, radiograph interpretation is typically taught as part of an anatomy course. Medical school students do have the option of taking a radiology elective, and there may be some exposure during an internal medicine or surgical clerkship.

It was reported in Britain in 2003 that final-year medical students were shown ten conventional chest radiographs that were good radiological examples of common conditions. "On no radiograph were more than 25% of students definite about their answer," and in general the students did "not perform well at interpreting simple chest radiographs" (Jeffrey).

The doctors in Grantville, of course, are not fresh out of medical school. However, that doesn't mean that they have substantial radiological expertise. A 2021 survey asked family medicine and radiology residents to interpret ten emergency chest X-rays with brief clinical information. The overall diagnostic accuracy was 58.0% for the former and 90.5% for the latter (Al-Shammari). Better performance was reported in a 1995 study of family physicians in an outpatient practice at a university hospital—89% of chest films were interpreted correctly, and 96% of extremity films (Bergus). A 1990 study (Halvorsen) of family physicians reported that when they referred films to a radiologist, the disagreement rate was 12.5%. Of course, the referral may have been made because the family physician lacked confidence in his or her own diagnosis.

Dental Radiography

Standard adult periapical and bitewing films are 31x41 mm, and occlusal films are 57x76 mm. Intensifying screens were not used for these exposures.

It is uncertain whether the dentists in Grantville have panoramic X-ray equipment, which has the means for holding the patient's head in a fixed position while the X-ray tube is rotated around the mouth. Although the equipment was on the market well before the Ring of Fire, my own first panoramic X-ray was at least two decades after it.

The table below should give some idea how dental and medical (general and CT) X-ray tubes compare nowadays:

Table 1: Comparison of Selected Modern Canon X-ray Tubes

	Focal Spot (mm)	Maximum Power Rating (W)	Tube Voltage (kVp)	Tube Current (mA)	Anode Heat Capacity (kJ)
dental intraoral DG-073B-DC	0.5	560 (1s)	70 (fixed)	8 (fixed)	7 stationary anode
mobile med DF-151	0.5 1.5	680 3200	110	15 60	28 stationary anode
medical general 3" tube E7894X	0.6 1.2	15,000 30,000 (0.1s)	150 (max)	200* 500* *max, also affected by set kVp	100 rotating anode (3200 rpm)
medical CT scanner E79005X	1.7 1.3	36,000 24,000 (2700 rpm)	80-135	300* 220* *max	1420 (2700 rpm)

(The medical tubes are at the low end of the respective canon lines, and the dental tube at the high end.)

Veterinary Radiography

Given the rural nature of Grantville, I would assume that the vet is examining large animals as well as pets. This imposes some constraints on the choice of X-ray equipment. First, either the equipment will be portable (so it can be taken to the animal) or it will be on an overhead crane. Second, the power rating must be high enough to penetrate the animal's anatomy (the modern Vet-Ray MX-2 mobile is 50,000 watts, with a maximum tube current of 500 milliamperes). Third, vets will need some large format X-ray film.

Portable Radiography

Very soon after the first radiograph of the human skeleton (1895), the military put portable X-ray machines into the field. In the Nile River War (1896-98), the British generated electricity by having two cyclists pedal a tandem bicycle. The rear wheel was connected to a dynamo, which in turn charged wet batteries (Eisenberg 31). The military surgeons were favorably impressed by the ease with which the radiogram revealed the location of a bullet inside the body.

The "radiological car"—essentially a car carrying the X-ray machine and the dynamo—was developed during World War I by Madame Curie and hence such cars were called "Little Curies" (Jorgensen).

A portable X-ray machine may be mounted on a hand truck (so it can be pushed) or it may be self-powered (by batteries).

Batteries may also be used to energize the tube itself. In that case, they probably are used to charge up capacitors which then are discharged into the tube. This would be combined with a grid-controlled tube, in which a negative voltage is applied between the focus-cup (grid) and the filament to prevent exposure until the capacitors reach the required kilovoltage. In addition, there is a lead shutter on the collimator to block premature emissions due to "dark-current" (McClelland 217).

X-ray Therapy

It is extremely unlikely that the X-ray equipment in Grantville has ever been used for radiation therapy, or that the general-practice physicians in Grantville have ever engaged in radiation therapy. They may, of course, have referred patients to the hospital in Fairmont for such therapy and have some knowledge of the treatment course.

EB15 indicates that X-rays are used to eradicate tumors, but provides no details as to the appropriate voltages. It does note the possibility of irradiating a deep tumor from different directions, and of administering a chemical that sensitizes the tumor to the radiation (EB15/Therapeutics/Radiation Therapy). Advanced imaging techniques (computerized tomography) may also be used to better visualize the tumor.

Some sense of the X-ray energies used in therapy may be gleaned by looking at the 1983 West Virginia radiological health regulations, as these have different rules depending on whether the X-ray therapy equipment is capable of operating at a peak voltage above or below 500 kilovolts (7.2(24)).

I do not know the peak voltage of the diagnostic X-ray equipment in Grantville, but the 1999 FDA Resource Manual for Compliance Test Parameters of Diagnostic X-ray Systems gave recommended aluminum-equivalent filtration values for peak tube voltages up to 150 kilovolts.

Superficial therapy can be carried out with voltages in the 50-150 kilo-volt range. More powerful therapeutic X-ray beams are variously classified as orthovoltage (150-500 kilovolts), supervoltage (500-1000 kilovolts), and megavoltage (1000 kilovolts up), which reach progressively deeper into the body (RadiologyKey).

Megavoltage X-ray Sources

Van de Graaff Generator

The first one, with a silk ribbon belt and a tin can accumulator, was constructed in 1929 and generated 80 kilovolts. The first clinical machine (about one megavolt) was installed in 1937 (Mould 18.23).

EB15 describes the components of a van de Graaff generator: a moving, insulated rubber belt, a large conducting metal dome, and two sets of electrodes (each a "comb of needles"). The belt is wrapped around two pulleys, one of which is inside the dome. According to the accompanying illustration, the lower electrodes, near the bottom pulley, are connected to the positive terminal of a voltage source ("a few tens of kilovolts"), and the upper electrodes, near the top pulley, to the dome. The lower electrodes positively charge the rising belt and the upper electrodes transfer the positive charge to the dome. If the generator is insulated with pres-surized gas, a potential of 20 megavolts can be achieved (EB15/Particle Accelerators; van de Graaff, Robert Jemison). The essay goes on to discuss the use of that potential to accelerate positively charged particles from an ion source through a vacuum tube. In passing, it is noted that a van de Graaff generator can also be used to accelerate electrons.

If one has two generators, and negative charges are delivered to the sphere of one and positive charges to the sphere of the other, the voltage difference can be doubled.

In the electron-accelerating, X-ray producing embodiment, the voltage source sprays electrons onto the bottom of the moving belt, which is driven by a motorized pulley. The electrons are carried up and collected onto the dome. "The X-ray tube is placed parallel to the belt, and consists of a filament at the top, a series of accelerating electrodes, and a water-cooled target at the bottom. The upper spherical electrode at a high negative potential is joined to ground by a series of high resistances." The whole device is inside a steel tank (Mould). The accelerating electrodes are in the form of a series of metal rings with resistors connecting the rings. The purpose of the resistors is to provide a uniform drop in potential from top to bottom. The insulating gas is typically a mixture of nitrogen and carbon dioxide (RadiologyKey).

There are a few practical issues with these generators. First, there is the issue of driving the belt quickly and reliably enough to charge the dome to the desired voltage in a reasonable time. The second is avoiding premature discharge (arcing). Dry air at standard temperature and pressure becomes conducting when subjected to an electric field of 30 kilovolts/centimeter. The maximum voltage achievable by the generator would then be the radius (centimeters) of the dome times thirty (Wikipedia). The maximum voltage may be increased either by increasing the radius of the dome or increasing the dielectric constant of the medium (surrounding the dome in a suitable liquid, pressurized gas, or vacuum). The support for the dome must also have a high dielectric constant.

The high school may have a tabletop van de Graaff generator (mine did). However, this might not use a voltage source. Rather, a charge separation is achieved by the triboelectric effect, the belt and the rollers being dissimilar materials. However, even with just the triboelectric effect, a voltage of 350 kilovolts is achievable. If you go that route, then to transport a negative charge, the lower pulley should be covered with or made of a material that is triboelectric positive (glass, felt, silk) and the upper pulley with one that is triboelectric negative (brass, celluloid, rayon, PVC). Natural rubber is in-between, though more negative than steel (SSE).

* * *

There are other ways of generating a megavoltage (e.g., a betatron) but the Van de Graaff generator seems the most readily achievable in the new timeline.

Industrial Radiography

Industrial radiography permits non-destructive inspection of products and engineering structures. It can be used for quality control in the manufacturing process, and periodic monitoring for the development of cracks and other flaws.

The targets of industrial radiography are typically metal alloys and thus attenuate X-rays much more strongly than does the human body. Often, they are thicker than the human body, too.

Hence, one must provide harder radiation (the degree of attenuation generally decreases with increasing photon energy) and/or higher intensity radiation (more photons per second per unit area), or increase exposure time, in order to obtain a usable image.

It is not unusual to use a high voltage electron tube as a source of hard radiation in a factory setting. However, in the field, a portable source is needed and often this is a radioactive material such as iridium-192 or cobalt-60. These emit gamma rays, which in general are even higher energy than X-rays and thus are also suitable for imaging thicker structures.

Industrial radiography is alluded to as an unavailable technology as of June 1637, at least in Saalfeld (Carroll and Wild, Love and Chemistry, Chapter 24).

X-ray Spectroscopy

When a high-energy X-ray photon strikes and is absorbed by an atom, an inner shell electron is ejected, and an outer shell electron takes its place. The highest absorption of X-rays by atoms of a particular element occurs when the energy of the X-ray photon is just above the binding energy of the inner shell electrons. The plot of absorption against energy will thus show a "K-edge" corresponding to the energy of the K-shell of the atom in question. The position of the K-edge identifies the element and the difference in absorption above and below the K-edge indicates the abundance of the element (EB15/Spectroscopy). Note that with larger atoms, there are also L-, M-, and even N-shells and corresponding edges, requiring progressively harder X-rays.

Since the outer-shell electron had a lower binding energy than the inner shell electron, the energy difference manifests itself by the emission (fluorescence) of a lower energy X-ray photon (a secondary X-ray). The energies of the secondary X-rays will also be characteristic of the atom in question (EB15/X Ray).

Until 1635, Grantville had a working portable X-ray fluorescence device (Metallurgist XR Model 9277) at the power plant ("Mente Et Malleo: Practical Mineralogy And Minerals Exploration In 1632," Runkle, Grantville Gazette 2). It had two components, the probe and the analyzer. The probe has two radioactive sealed sources, iron-55 and cadmium-109. "A high resolution mercuric iodide X-ray detector" reads 21 different elements and the analyzer determines their percentages (Funk).

Iron-55 has a half-life of 2.737 years and cadmium-109 of 461.4 days. It is the decay of these sources, and consequent deterioration in sensitivity, that is the cause of the loss of functionality of this device.

There is no reasonable prospect for production of either isotope in the new 1630s. Cadmium-109 was produced in nuclear reactors by neutron irradiation of silver, and in particle accelerators by proton bombardment of indium.

However, while portable XRF devices use radioisotopes, laboratory instruments employ a 50-60 kV X-ray tube (LightAnalytics). While that is doable, a compatible detector would also need to be developed, and the electronics for interpreting the detector output.

X-ray Crystallography

In a crystal, there is a regular, repeating arrangement of atoms. Atoms in a crystal are spaced a few angstroms apart. X-rays have wavelengths covering that size range; hence, the directional dependence of the scattering of X-rays by the crystal can be used to discern the atomic arrangement. Depending on the positions of the atoms, the scattered waves from different atoms may reinforce each other or cancel each other out, creating a "diffraction pattern." Since X-rays are scattered as a result of interactions with the electrons, they are best suited to detecting atoms of high atomic number (EB15/crystal).

While not explained by EB15, the crystal will be mounted on a goniometer so its orientation relative to a fixed X-ray beam may be changed, preferably on several axes of rotation. A series of diffraction patterns are obtained, each from a slightly different direction.

There are several problems with using X-ray crystallography to characterize a chemical in the new timeline. First, for analysis to be possible, it must be obtained in the form of a large, pure crystal. Second, the X-ray beam must be monochromatic (so a suitable filter is needed) and collimated (the waves travelling in the same direction). Third, it must be centered on the crystal. Fourth, the rotations of the crystal must be precise. Fifth, considerable computation is needed to go from the set of diffraction patterns to a hypothetical structure. In some cases it may be necessary to postulate a structure, calculate how the X-rays would scatter from it, and then compare the hypothetical diffraction patterns to the observed ones. The more complicated the chemical, the more possibilities exist.

It would not surprise me if, within a couple of years after the first new timeline X-ray tubes were made, there were some sort of "proof of concept" experiment: purifying and crystallizing a simple chemical (sodium chloride for example, determined in 1914) and then confirming that the inferred structure matches the known one (assuming the structure is given in Grantville literature, which isn't a sure thing).

News and New Books
Available Now and Coming Soon

Flint's Shards, Inc.

Available Now

1635: The Weaver's Code, 1635: Music and Murder, The Private Casefiles of Archie Gottesfreund, The Trouble with Huguenots, Things Could be Worse, Designed to Fail, The Unexpected Sales Reps

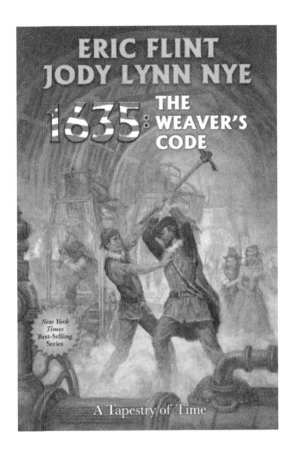

1635: The Weaver's Code
Eric Flint and Jody Lynn Nye

A young gentlewoman, Margaret de Beauchamp, finds her fate twisted into the lives of the up-timers when she meets the Americans imprisoned in the Tower of London. In exchange for her help, Rita Simpson and Harry Lefferts give her a huge sum of money to keep her family's manor and its woolen trade from falling into the hands of the crown and its unscrupulous minister, Lord Cork. But Margaret's troubles are not at an end. Her family's fortunes are in a downward spiral. Her trip to Grantville brings unexpected dangers and a possible up-time solution.

Inspired by books in the Grantville library, Margaret has an idea to restore her family's fortunes with an innovation never before seen in fabric design. With the help of Aaron Craig, an up-timer programmer using aqualators, water-powered computers, they teach her father's craftsmen to create a combination machine loom that can produce a new type of woolen cloth. The ornate and perfect patterns quickly trend among the nobility. However, the Master Weavers of the county's Weaver's Guild aren't happy about being overshadowed by the changes to the status quo, and take their grievance to Lord Cork, who is still looking for the people who helped the Americans escape from the Tower.

Cork isn't interested in squabbles between mere tradesmen, but he is very interested in taking over the new calculating machine that is fueling the upsurge in the de Beauchamp fortunes. He sends agents ordered to stop at nothing to secure it for his own ends. Margaret has to protect her new business, and prevent anyone from discovering that up-timers are in the country to assist her, but she still has to deal with an uprising at home.

https://www.baen.com/1635-the-weaver-s-code.html

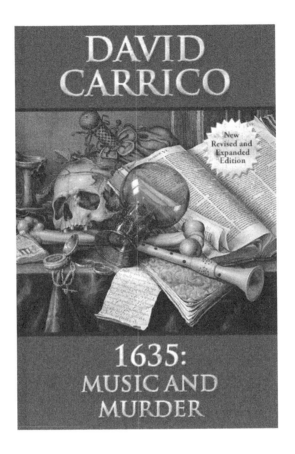

1635: Music and Murder
David Carrico

Music . . .

It's been said that musicians live for the next new sound. Well, the musicians of Europe were presented with the biggest new sound ever when the Ring of Fire brought the future back to 1631. What will the court musicians think when they hear Bach, Stravinsky, and the Beatles? What will the street and tavern musicians think when faced with Johnny Cash, Metallica, and Nirvana? Things don't go smoothly for Marla Linder and her friends.

And Murder . . .

The Thirty Years War was an 'interesting' time to be alive, in the proverbial Chinese curse sense of the word. Then Grantville arrived from the future, bringing technology and philosophies that set European civilization on its ear. But that's not all that came back with Grantville. Imagine trying to establish modern police procedures in a time where neither the powers-that-be nor the people underneath them provide much support. Up-timer Byron Chieske and his down-timer partner Gotthilf Hoch walk some mean streets and lonely roads.

This is an updated edition with "Canticle de Noël." This was originally published in *A 1632 Christmas* and has been moved here so that all the Marla and Franz stories are in one place. This edition also contains an Author's Afterward.

https://www.baen.com/1635-music-and-murder.html

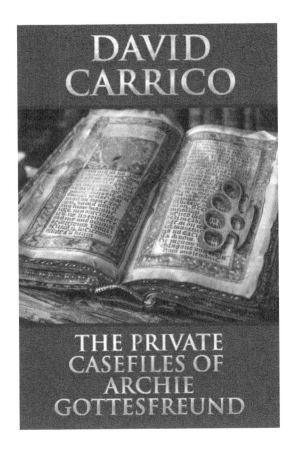

The Private Casefiles of Archie Gottesfreund
David Carrico

New detective and adventure stories laid in the Ring of Fire Universe.

Archibald Gottesfreund, a half-Scot/half-German mercenary, retired from that life after losing both his cousin Rory and part of his own left hand in a skirmish with brigands in northern France. Weary of that life, Archie rode east, looking for a new life, which he found in Jena when he met up with Master Tiberius Claudius Titus Wulff. After doing the master merchant a favor, he found himself enlisted to be Master Titus' chief agent and right-hand man, a life he never expected.

Over the years, Master Titus' business affairs and his passion for books alike provide many adventures for Archie. Two of the best are presented in this volume.

https://www.baen.com/the-private-casefiles-of-archie-gottesfreund.html

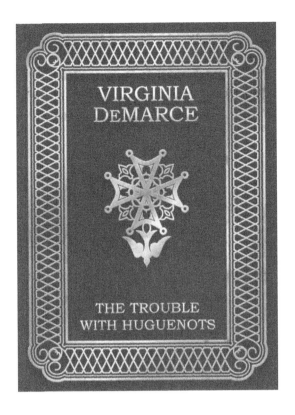

The Trouble with Huguenots
Virginia DeMarce

Ever since the assassination of King Louis XIII and the overthrow of his chief minister, Cardinal Richelieu, France has been in political and military turmoil. The possibility—even the likelihood—of revolution hovers in the background. The new king, Gaston, whom many consider a usurper, is no friend of France's Protestants, known as the Huguenots. The fears and hostility of the Huguenots toward the French crown have only been heightened by the knowledge brought back in time by the Americans of the town of Grantville. Half a century in the future, the French king of the time would revoke the Edict of Nantes of 1598, which proclaimed that the rights of Huguenots would be respected. At the center of all this turmoil is the universally recognized leader of the Huguenots: Duke Henri de Rohan. He knows from the same up-time history books that he is "scheduled" to die less than two years in the future and he has pressing problem on his hands. His estranged wife and brother are siding with the usurper Gaston and plotting against him. Still worse, his sole child and heir is his nineteen-year-old daughter Marguerite. He believes he has less than two years to find a suitable husband for her—but acceptable Calvinist noblemen, French or foreign, are sparse at the moment. What's a father to do?

https://www.baen.com/the-trouble-with-huguenots-demarce.html

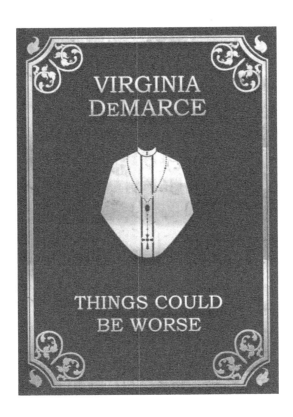

Things Could Be Worse
Virginia DeMarce

The Ring of Fire that transported the town of Grantville from West Virginia in the year 2000 to the region of Thuringia in the middle of Europe in the year 1631 produced an enormous cascade of changes in world history. Some of those changes were big, others were huge—and some were more modest in scale. Modest, at the least, to the universe, if not necessarily to those immediately affected.

Count Ludwig Guenther of Schwarzburg-Rudolstadt builds a Lutheran church on his own land, not far from Grantville, and calls in a Saxon pastor of a Philippist bent to serve the Lutheran refugee population of the area. Shortly thereafter, in April 1634, the pastor's older daughter meets and elopes with a Catholic up-timer, which prompts Kastenmayer to get Lutheran girls to marry unchurched up-timers and thereby recruit them into the parish.

In the years that follow, Pastor Kastenmayer copes with both existing ecclesio-political strands of down-time religion (from Stiefelite Lutheran heretics to Flacian Lutheran ultra-orthodox) and the strange new up-time world of shorts, blue jeans, and unknown religious denominations. His struggles and travails have a surprisingly revolutionary impact on seventeenth-century Lutheranism—perhaps to no one's greater surprise than the pastor himself.

https://www.baen.com/things-could-be-worse-demarce.html

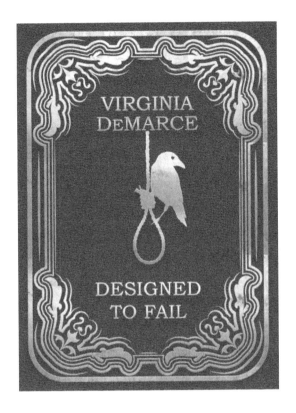

Designed To Fail
Virginia DeMarce

Frederik of Denmark, the son of King Christian IV, is the new governor of the new province of Westphalia and harbors the dark suspicion that the Swedes who now dominate central Europe deliberately designed the province so that he would not succeed in his assignment, thus undermining his father's position. Problems are everywhere! Religious fragmentation, cities demanding imperial status, jurisdictional disputes among the nobility and between the nobility and the common folk—there's no end to it.

And then matters get still more complicated. Annalise Richter, a student at the famous Abbey of Quedlinburg, wants Frederik to correct an injustice. Her mentor, the Abbess of Quedlinburg, is being prevented from running for a seat in the House of Commons because she is, well, not a commoner. Surely Frederik can do something to fix this wrong! The prince is of two minds. On the one hand—being very much his father's son—he has developed a great passion for the marvelous young woman. He is determined to marry her. On the other hand . . . she's Catholic. A bit of a problem, that, for a Lutheran prince. But there's worse. She's also the younger sister of Gretchen Richter. Yes, that Gretchen Richter.

https://www.baen.com/designed-to-fail.html

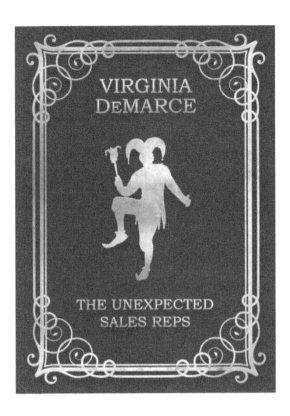

The Unexpected Sales Reps
Virginia DeMarce

How to succeed at spying without really trying.

Pranksters and scammers from way back, Paolo Fucilla and Carlo Rigatti fought for Spain at the Wartburg and survived.

Curious about the people who had beaten them so handily, they went to Grantville. Whatever their other faults, they were serious about keeping their oaths. When they promised not to take up arms they meant it. In Grantville, they got in trouble again and skipped town.

Looking for a job that didn't include being shot at with napalm, they decided to try their hand at spying. It was a "Here, hold my beer and watch this" inspiration. It wasn't their first, and it wouldn't be their last.

They went to work for the Archbishop of Salzburg. But spies need cover stories, so they decided to sell office supplies. It was supposed to be a single job, so they didn't bother to tell the manufacturer that they were now the sales reps for Vignelli Business Machines.

Watch as Paolo and Carlo demonstrate the kind of trouble they can get into.

https://www.baen.com/september-ebook-tbd.html

Coming Soon

1637: The French Correction, 1637: The Pacific Initiative, Letters from Gronow, Magdeburg Noir

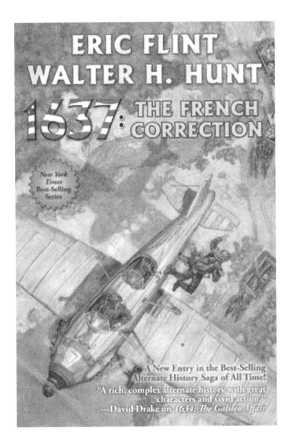

1637: The French Correction
By Eric Flint & Walter Hunt

NEW RING OF FIRE SERIES ENTRY FROM THE LATE ERIC FLINT AND BEST-SELLING AUTHOR WALTER HUNT: The King is dead: Long Live the King. But which one? Gaston sits on the throne in Paris, but the dead king's infant son has powerful forces on his side, ready to place him where he belongs. Who will prevail?

Tensions build in France following the ascension of Gaston to the throne of his murdered brother, but there are factions supporting the claim of King Louis' surviving infant son. As France moves toward civil war, other parties, both visible and invisible, maneuver to take advantage of the increased tension. Who will survive to reign over France—King Gaston, the exiled child and his regents, or the King of Spain?

Coming March 4, 2025

Baen Monthly Ebook Bundle:

https://www.baen.com/w202503-march-2025-monthly-bundle.html

Baen monthly ebook bundles are available until the day before official publication. Half of each book is available three months ahead of time, and three-quarters two months ahead of time. These are pre-final proofreads.

e-ARC:

This is the electronic Advance Reader's Copy. It is not the final production version.

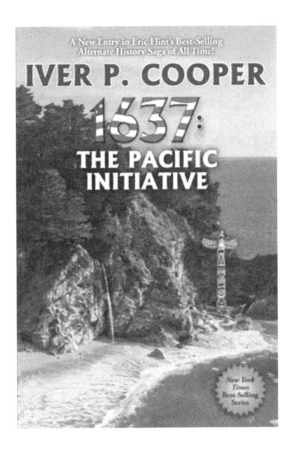

1637: The Pacific Initiative
Iver P. Cooper

NEW RING OF FIRE SERIES ENTRY FROM IVER P. COOPER

A cosmic catastrophe, the Ring of Fire, strands the West Virginia town of Grantville back in time in the middle of the Thirty Years War. One of its ripple effects is that Japan has pulled back from a policy of isolation and staked out its own claims on the west coast of North America. But it is not the only power interested in that part of the New World, and the native Americans have also responded, in different ways, to the unexpected colonists. And there are conflicts among the colonists themselves.

In settling the fate of this part of the New World, a few remarkable individuals have an outsize role to play: Oyamada Isamu, a samurai on his first independent command; Yells-at-Bears, a young native woman of Vancouver Island; Father Blanco, a Jesuit priest and former missionary; and Iroha Date-hime, the daughter of the Grand Governor of New Nippon.

Coming March 4, 2025

Baen Monthly Ebook Bundle:

https://www.baen.com/w202503-march-2025-monthly-bundle.html

Baen monthly ebook bundles are available until the day before official publication. Half of each book is available three months ahead of time, and three-quarters two months ahead of time. These are pre-final proofreads.

https://www.baen.com/1637-the-pacific-initiative-earc.html

This is the electronic Advance Reader's Copy. It is not the final production version.

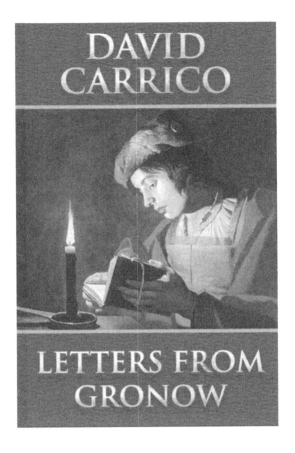

Letters from Gronow
David Carrico

What happens when the seventeenth century encounters Cthulhu and Nyarlathotep? What happens when the Elder Gods descend upon Magdeburg? When literary entrepreneur Johann Gronow discovers the stories of H. P. Lovecraft and Edgar Allen Poe in the libraries and book collections of Grantville, he launches a magazine for the purpose of publishing translations of their stories. Der Schwarze Kater—The Black Tomcat—begins attracting attention immediately. From his very first reading of the first issue of the magazine, a young bookkeeper named Philip Fröhlich develops a passion to write those kinds of stories. And so begins the quest of every author—to satisfy the requirements of an editor and make that first elusive sale. As have millions of aspiring authors, Philip discovers it's not as easy as it looks. Time after time his submissions receive a rejection letter from Gronow. But Philip stubbornly keeps submitting, along the way discovering things about himself and the people around him that he never would have learned any other way.

Published: 2/4/2025

Baen Monthly Ebook Bundle:

https://www.baen.com/w202502-february-2025-monthly-baen-bundle.html

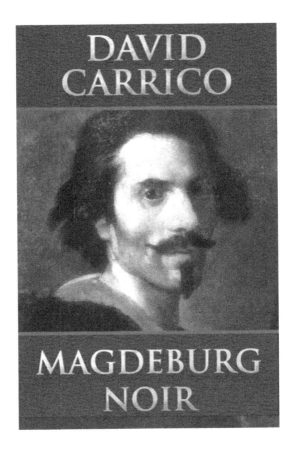

Magdeburg Noir
David Carrico

Magdeburg, the capital of the newly-formed United States of Europe, has a dark and bloody history. Most of the city and its population were destroyed when the imperialist army ran amok after capturing the city in May of 1631. The ancient Gothic cathedral was one of the few structures that survived more-or-less intact.

Once the Swedish king Gustav Adolf drove out the imperialists and established the USE, Magdeburg began to recover—and then grow at an astonishing rate. New industries inspired by the technology of the time-transplanted Americans of Grantville are turning the city into a boom town, with immigrants from all over central Europe pouring in.

A boom town is full of hope and aspiration—but it's also a place that generates its own darkness and chaos. The city's fledgling police force is scrambling to get control over the growing crime and violence. Sometimes it succeeds—but often it doesn't. And such failures bring down the might of the city's powerful revolutionary Committees of Correspondence, whose leader Gunther Achterhof can match any criminal's ruthlessness.

Musicians murdered, new and brutal religious cults arising, bombings and arson, spies and informers and those hunting them—these are only some of the ingredients in the reborn city of light and darkness.

Published: 2/4/2025

Baen Monthly Ebook Bundle:

https://www.baen.com/w202502-february-2025-monthly-baen-bundle.html

Connect with Eric Flint's 1632 & Beyond

We would love to hear from you here at *Eric Flint's 1632 & Beyond!* There are lots of ways to get in touch with us and we look forward to hearing from you.

Main Sites

Email: 1632Magazine@1632Magazine.com

Shop: 1632Magazine.com

Author Site: Author.1632Magazine.com

For anyone interested in writing in the 1632verse, or fans interested in more background on the series and how we keep track of everything.

Social Media

Our Facebook Group is our primary social media, but we do use the FB Page, YouTube, and Instagram accounts.

Facebook Group: The Grantville Gazette / 1632 & Beyond

YouTube: 1632andBeyond

Facebook Page: Facebook.com/t1632andBeyond

Reviews and More

Because reviews really do matter, especially for small publishers and indie authors, please take a few minutes to post a review online or wherever you find books, and don't forget to tell your friends to check us out!

You are welcome to join us on **BaensBar.net**. Most of the chatting about 1632 on the Bar is in the 1632 Tech forum. If you want to read and comment on possible future stories, check out 1632 Slush (stories) and 1632 Slush Comments on BaensBar.net.

If you are interested in writing in the 1632 universe, that's fabulous! Please visit **Author.1632Magazine.com** (QR code above) for more information.

Made in the USA
Las Vegas, NV
22 February 2025

18537359R00134